fairy

fairy

Belinda Ray

SCHOLASTIC INC.
New York Toronto London Auckland Sydney
Mexico City New Delhi Hong Kong Buenos Aires

For Ward, who speaks a language all his own
—B.R.

ISBN 0-439-56013-6

Copyright © 2004 by 17th Street Productions,
an Alloy company
All rights reserved.
Published by Scholastic Inc.

Produced by 17th Street Productions,
an Alloy company
151 West 26th Street
New York, NY 10001

12 11 10 9 8 7 6 5 4 3 2 1   4 5 6 7 8 9/0

Printed in the U.S.A.   40
First printing, January 2004

fairy

CHAPTER
One

"Resa! Do you have my silver hoops?" Amy Allen called, leaning through her sister's bedroom door. "You know, the ones I loaned you last week?"

Theresa winced. "Um, I don't think so," she replied, squinting her big brown eyes. "Are you sure I didn't give them back?"

Amy shook her head. "I just checked my jewelry box, and they're not in there. And I loaned them to you over a week ago."

"Maybe you put them somewhere else," Theresa suggested. Her sister groaned.

"Unlike you," Amy said, "I put my things back where they belong. If my earrings aren't in my jewelry box, then I don't have them, which means *you do.* So cough 'em up."

Theresa glanced around her room, her eyes

darting to every spot where it would have made sense to set earrings—her nightstand, her bureau, her desk. *"Well,"* she said slowly. She tugged on one of her long brown braids and twisted it around her finger nervously. She willed herself to remember where she'd put them, but the memory wouldn't come.

Amy folded her arms across her chest. "You lost my earrings, didn't you?"

"No-o."

"Then where are they?"

Theresa sighed. "I'm not sure."

"Resa! Those were my favorite—"

"I'll find them, Amy. I just—"

"Theresa! Amy! Breakfast!" Mr. Allen called from downstairs.

Amy gave her sister one last glare. "You better," she said. Then she turned and headed downstairs.

Phew, Theresa thought. *Saved by the bacon.*

She took one last look around her room and shook her head. Where had she put those stupid earrings? Oh, well. She'd have to solve that mystery later. Theresa snagged her backpack from the chair at her desk and headed for the kitchen, where her mother, father, and eight-year-old brother, Nicky, were already seated around the table.

"So," Mr. Allen began, once Theresa had taken her seat, "do you kids have anything interesting going on in school this week?"

"We're starting our clay sculptures in art class today," Nicky said. He chomped on a muffin, and crumbs spilled all over the table. "I'm not sure what I'm going to make yet."

"Well, I'm sure you'll think of something really inventive, Nicky," Mrs. Allen said. "What about you girls? Anything fun happening at school?"

"Not really," Amy said, rolling her eyes. "I'm probably going to go shopping after school today with Stephanie. You know, because I guess I *need some new earrings.*"

"Oh," said Mrs. Allen. "You girls enjoy that. What about you, Theresa?"

Theresa brightened up a little despite Amy's earring comment. "We're going to start planning the spring carnival."

Mrs. Allen knit her brow. "Is it time for that already?" she asked.

"Duh," Amy said, rolling her eyes. "It *is* spring."

"Amy, don't talk to me that way," Mrs. Allen said.

"Sorry," Amy said sheepishly. "I just meant

that it's April, and Resa's class did their play about two weeks ago, which means it's time for spring carnival. Middle school is *so* predictable."

"So are sophomores with crushes," Theresa muttered under her breath. Then, when her sister glared at her, she mouthed the name *Chip.* Theresa had overheard Amy on the phone last night, telling one of her friends all about her huge crush on some guy named Chip.

"Excuse me?" Mrs. Allen asked.

Amy reached over and pinched Theresa hard on the thigh. "*Ow*—nothing," Theresa said. "I was just saying that I'm really excited. I hope my class wins the ice cream party."

Amy raised her juice glass and looked Theresa in the eye. "You won't," she said. Then she took a long sip of orange juice.

"Amy, that's not very supportive," Mrs. Allen said.

Amy half shrugged. "Maybe not, but it's true," she replied. "The fifth grade *never* wins. It's practically tradition."

"Just because your fifth grade didn't win doesn't mean mine can't," Theresa said.

"It wasn't just *my* fifth grade that didn't win," Amy replied. "*No* fifth grade has ever won. *Ever.*"

"Really?" Theresa asked.

"If you don't believe me, check the trophy cases by the office. There's a list of every class that's ever won, and there's not a single fifth grade on it."

Theresa narrowed her eyes. That didn't seem right, but why would Amy lie? Especially when she knew Theresa could check.

"Well, then, perhaps Theresa's class will be the first," Mr. Allen said. "More muffins, anyone?" He held up the plate. Theresa, Amy, and Mrs. Allen all shook their heads.

"Yeah, right," Amy said. "If Theresa has anything to do with it, they'll misplace their theme."

"What?!" Theresa exclaimed.

"It's true—you'd lose your feet if they weren't attached to your ankles."

"Amy—that was uncalled for," Mrs. Allen chided her. "Apologize to your sister, please."

"*Sor-ry,*" Amy whined in a singsong voice.

Theresa waited until her mother wasn't looking and then stuck out her tongue.

"Real mature," Amy murmured. She folded her napkin and set it on the table, then stood to take her plate to the sink. At the same time, Mr. and Mrs. Allen stood to clear the table. Theresa gulped down the last bite of her muffin and took her plate up, too.

"We're going to win, you know," Theresa said while she waited for her sister to finish rinsing her plate.

"Mm-hm," Amy replied without turning around. "And winged monkeys are going to come live under my bed."

Theresa clicked her tongue. "Why do you have to be so rude?"

"I'm not rude. I'm just honest," Amy said. "There's no way your class is going to win. I already told you—the fifth grade never wins. Get over it already." She opened the dishwasher, placed her plate on the bottom rack, and walked away, leaving Theresa standing there fuming.

So the fifth grade had never won spring carnival before. So what? That didn't mean Theresa's class couldn't do it. And if it meant proving Amy wrong, Theresa was going to make sure that they did!

CHAPTER

Two

"I brought 'The Lion and the Mouse,'" said Anna Lee, removing a sheet of paper from her notebook. For English class Mrs. Wessex was having the fifth graders research Aesop's fables. They were working in groups of three, and each student was responsible for finding one fable to share.

"Which one is that?" Theresa asked.

Anna pushed her straight, jet-black hair back behind her ears as she glanced up from her work. "It's the one where the lion catches a mouse but lets him go," she said. "Then the mouse helps him later by chewing a hole in the net the lion is caught in."

"Oh—I know that one," Carrie Weingarten replied. "The moral is something like 'Small creatures can do big things,' right?"

"That's the one," Anna said. "So what did you guys bring?"

"I have 'The Fox and the Grapes,'" Carrie said, removing her own sheet of notebook paper on which she'd copied down her fable. "It's about a fox that wants some grapes that are growing up high, but he can't reach them. He tries and tries to get them, but he can't. So finally he just walks away and says that he could tell they were sour anyway."

"I've heard that one before," Theresa said, twirling several of her tiny braids around her finger, "but I don't really get it. What's the moral supposed to be?"

Anna grinned and leaned in close, her dark, almond-shaped eyes sparkling. "It's about being a sore loser," she whispered. "You know, like when Sharon doesn't get her way and then pretends she's better off anyway?"

Carrie giggled. "Right. Like the time we beat her in the math contest and she said it didn't matter because she was getting tired of winning free ice cream."

Theresa smiled, remembering how thrilled she and her friends had been to win—and how upset Sharon had been to lose. Sharon Ross preferred to come in first. At everything.

"That must be where the expression 'sour grapes' comes from," she said. "My dad's always saying that to my brother when he says Monopoly or whatever is a stupid game . . . *right after he loses*."

"I've heard him do that before," Carrie said. "Nicky is cute and I love him and all that, but he can be so whiny."

"Tell me about it," Theresa said. "You guys are lucky you don't have little brothers. They can be such a pain."

"Trust me," Anna said, "big brothers can be just as bad."

"And so can big sisters," Carrie added. "But then, I guess you know that."

Theresa nodded. Amy was definitely as big a pain as Nicky—sometimes bigger.

"So what fable did you bring, Theresa?" Anna asked.

"Oh, yeah," Theresa said. "Hold on a second, it's right here." She began to fumble through her backpack, searching for the page she'd printed out last night. "It's a really good one," she said. "'The Fox and the . . . Sheep'? No, that wasn't it. It's—" She tried to remember the other animal from the fable while she rifled through all of the loose papers inside her backpack.

"Was it 'The Fox and the Crow'?" Anna suggested.

"No," Theresa said without looking up. "It wasn't a bird. Wait a minute—I think it's in my notebook." Theresa removed a blue, spiral-bound notebook that was overflowing with various work sheets and printouts.

"Whoa," Carrie said. "I hope it's not in there."

Theresa glanced up. "Why not?" she asked.

"Because if it is, you'll never find it," Anna answered. Both she and Carrie were staring wide-eyed at the mess Theresa was making as she piled more and more papers onto her desk.

Theresa rolled her eyes. "Don't worry—I'll clean it all up once I find my fable," she said. "I know it's in here somewhere." She held the notebook by its front and back covers and shook it over her desk. A ton of papers fell out, and Theresa examined every one, but her fable was nowhere to be found.

Anna grimaced. "Theresa, maybe you should just—"

"Let me check one more place," Theresa said, holding up an index finger to her friends.

"Was it 'The Fox and the Stork'?" Carrie suggested. "I saw that one online at Aesop.com."

"*No-o*," Theresa said. "I told you it wasn't a bird."

"What about 'The Fox and the Monkey'?" Anna asked. "I almost did that one."

Theresa groaned. "No, it wasn't a monkey, either. Just wait and I'll find it." She began unzipping all of the pockets on her backpack.

The first one was empty. The second one held her calculator. "Hey, I've been looking for that," Theresa mumbled, setting it on the desk. The third pocket contained a note that she, Carrie, and Anna had been writing back and forth during math class yesterday, and the last pocket, which was really too small to hold much of anything, had a quarter and three pennies.

"Shoot!" Theresa said, slouching forward. Amy was right. She couldn't keep track of anything. Theresa shook her head. "I swear I printed it out and stuck it in here last night so that I wouldn't forget it."

"Maybe it fell out," Carrie offered, shrugging.

"Or maybe you *meant* to put it in your backpack, but you forgot," Anna added.

"Hmmm," Theresa said. "Maybe." She frowned. "Man, I hate forgetting things. It was a really good fable, too—one I'd never heard before. That's why I chose it."

"Well," Carrie said, her hazel eyes full of hope, "maybe we can help you remember it."

"I'm sure we can," Anna agreed. Again she tucked a few stray strands of shiny black hair behind her ears. It was her getting-down-to-business move. "We already know it has a fox and one other animal, right?" she asked. Theresa nodded. "Do you remember anything else about it?"

Theresa closed her eyes and pursed her lips. "Let's see . . . The fox was stuck in a well." She opened her eyes and smiled. Slowly the details of the fable were coming back to her.

"What else?" Anna asked.

"Well, the other animal—whatever it was—came along and asked the fox what he was doing at the bottom of the well. Really he'd fallen in and gotten trapped, but he told the other animal that he was down there drinking the water because it was the best water ever. So the other animal, who was really thirsty, jumped in, too. Then the fox climbed on its back to get out and left it stuck in the well."

"Is that it?" Anna asked.

Theresa shrugged. "I think so."

"Well, that's good," Carrie said. "It sounds like you remember the whole thing. So all you need to do is write down what you just told us and hand it in to Mrs. Wessex as your fable."

"I guess," Theresa said. "Except that I don't remember the other animal or what the moral was."

"Maybe we can figure it out," suggested Anna.

"Figure what out?" someone asked.

Theresa turned around to see her friend Spence looking over her shoulder. He was in the group right next to her, Carrie, and Anna, with his friends Matt Dana and Kevin Hathaway.

"Are you guys done?" Matt asked, nodding in their direction.

"Almost," Anna said. "We're just trying to figure out Theresa's fable."

Kevin scrunched up his eyebrows, which were barely visible through the curly dark hair that was perpetually in his eyes. "Figure it out? Which one is it?" he asked.

"That's the problem," Theresa said, sighing. "I can't remember. I printed it out last night, but I left it at home, and now I can't remember. It's about a fox stuck in a well and some other animal that he tricks into helping him out."

"Hey—I know that one," Matt said. "It's 'The Fox and the Goat.'"

Theresa sat up suddenly. She felt like a light had gone on inside her head. "The goat! That's it!" she said. "Now I remember. Matt's right—it's 'The Fox and the Goat,' and when the fox gets out of the well, he refuses to help the goat, even though he promised he would. Then when the goat complains, the fox says something like, 'Well, you shouldn't have gotten in without knowing how to get out.' And *that's* the moral."

"The sly fox said to the goat down deep / next time fella, better look before you leap," Spence rapped.

Carrie smiled and shook her head, sending her red curls bouncing.

"Right," Theresa said, grinning. "Look before you leap. That's it exactly. Thanks, Spence. Thanks, Matt."

"No problem," the two boys replied at the same time.

"Then we're done," Carrie said. "Resa just needs to write that one down, and then we can start on the next part of the assignment."

"The next part?" Theresa asked.

"It's right here on the work sheet Mrs. Wessex gave us," Anna said.

Theresa combed through all the papers littering her desk, but the work sheet wasn't among them. "I must have left that at home, too," she said with a sigh.

"You can share mine," Anna said. She slid a piece of paper halfway between her and Theresa and read from it. "'Part two: When you've finished discussing your fables, choose one to present to the rest of the class in a creative manner.'"

"*In a creative manner?*" Carrie repeated, squinting.

"There are some suggestions here," Anna said. "We could turn it into a poem, draw pictures to illustrate it—"

"Or you could turn it into a rap," Spence cut in. "Hit it, Kev."

Right on cue, Kevin started beat boxing, making all sorts of drumlike noises with his mouth and hands. After a few beats Spence jumped in.

"The hare and the tortoise, they started to race / and that hare was laughing at the turtle's slow pace. / He ran up one hill and down the next, / then decided to chill and have a rest. / But the turtle kept chugging and passed right by / that crazy hare who thought he was so fly / and when Hare woke up, he was in disgrace / 'cause slow and steady Tortoise had won the race."

Spence ended his rap with his hands crossed and tucked into his armpits, his thumbs pointing upward.

Carrie laughed and clapped. "That's awesome, Spence!"

"Carrie Weingarten and Ward Willis," Mrs. Wessex called from her desk. She always used Spence's real first name, even though he'd told her over and over to call him Spence, which was short for his middle name, Spencer. "Are the two of you working?"

"Just practicing our presentations, Mrs. W.," Spence said with a grin. At the same time, Carrie gave Mrs. Wessex her best wide-eyed, innocent look.

Sure enough, Mrs. Wessex's features softened into a smile, as they always did when she was dealing with Spence. "All right," she said. "Just keep the noise down, please."

Carrie nodded at her teacher, then turned back to Spence. "She loves you, you know," she whispered.

"What's not to love?" Spence said with a shrug.

Anna sighed. *"Please,"* she said. "Anyway, your rap was really good," she added. "Is that what you guys are going to do?"

"Something like that," Spence said. "We

gotta get Matt in on the beat boxing, though."

"Or not," Matt said.

"Come on, Matt—you have to do *something*," Anna told him.

"Oh, I'll do something," Matt said. "Just not that. These two can handle the music," he said, gesturing at Spence and Kevin. "I'll take care of the visuals."

"That's right—you draw really well, don't you?" Anna said.

Matt shrugged. "I don't know about *really well*," he said, running one hand through his shaggy blond hair, "but I definitely draw better than I beat box."

Anna giggled, then turned back to Carrie and Theresa. "Speaking of visuals, we need to come up with some for *our* presentation. Which fable do you guys want to do, anyway?"

"I like Resa's," Carrie said. "Are you just about finished with it?"

"Yep," Theresa said, scribbling down the last few words. She'd been writing so fast, her hand was beginning to cramp.

"So then let's do that one," Anna said. " 'The Fox and the Goat.' How do you guys want to present it?"

"I know," Theresa said. "I'll be the goat. Carrie

can be the fox—because of her red hair—and Anna, you can be the narrator. We'll set up some chairs in a circle to be the well, and then we'll act it out. It will only take me a minute to rewrite it as a play."

Without hesitation, Theresa ripped a blank sheet of paper from her notebook and began writing again. She stopped when she realized her friends were both staring at her. *"What?"*

"It's just . . ." Carrie started.

"That was so quick," Anna said. "I mean, you got the idea like—"

"Lightning fast," Spence jumped in. "Yo—Tee leaves stuff home and gets all fretful / but she's so creative, no one minds that she's forgetful."

Anna and Carrie laughed, but Theresa felt her face getting hot. Being disorganized and absentminded weren't exactly the things she wanted to be known for. Unfortunately, they seemed to be two of the things people noticed most about her.

Her sister was always on her case for forgetting to relay phone messages, among other things—*like losing earrings*, Theresa thought. And her mom was constantly reminding her that she needed to be more organized so she wouldn't misplace things so often. Even Nicky had started bragging that his room was neater than Theresa's, and he was only eight.

Theresa sighed. It seemed like she was constantly being told how mixed up and forgetful she was. Of course, this was the first time anyone had rapped about it.

"Well?" she asked, looking to her friends. "Is it okay?"

"Is what okay?" Anna and Carrie said together.

"My idea—presenting the fable as a mini-play."

"Oh—yeah, it's great," Anna said. "I was just surprised by how fast you came up with it."

"Me too," Carrie said. "Spence is right. You *are* really creative."

"Thanks," Theresa said, although she couldn't help wondering why Carrie and Anna seemed so surprised. She'd always been creative, hadn't she? Why did it seem like her friends were just realizing it?

Probably because all they see when they look at me is how disorganized and absentminded I am, Theresa thought. Just like everybody else. She fingered the charm bracelet Carrie had given to her a couple of weeks ago when she'd been having a particularly bad day. She'd managed to lose her sneakers, break a picture frame, and mess up the flowers for the school play, all in the space of ten minutes.

According to Carrie and Anna, the bracelet had brought each of them good luck. They'd passed it on to Theresa, saying that it looked like she could use a little good luck, too, but so far it didn't seem to be working. In fact, Theresa was beginning to think she should give the bracelet back to Carrie before it ended up with Amy's earrings—lost.

"Resa—are you okay?" Carrie asked.

"Yeah," Theresa lied. "I just—"

"All right, class," Mrs. Wessex called out. She stood up from her desk and walked to the front of the room. "We're just about out of time. You can finish up with your fables at the beginning of class tomorrow, and then we'll start the presentations. Oh, and don't forget—after lunch, the whole fifth grade is meeting back here for a class discussion of spring carnival."

Whispers of excitement shot around the room. Spring carnival was one of the most anticipated events of the year at Elizabeth Cady Stanton Middle School.

"Settle down, everybody," Mrs. Wessex said. "We don't have time to discuss the details right now. Just remember to come back here after lunch and be ready to be creative—we're going to try to come up with an idea for our class theme."

Just as Mrs. Wessex finished speaking, the bell rang, and everyone was on their feet.

"Did you hear that, Tee?" Spence said, nudging her as they walked out of the room. "We need your creativity."

Theresa smiled. True, Spence had rapped about her forgetfulness just a few minutes ago, but at least he was focusing on the creative part now.

"We sure do," Kevin added. Then he turned to Carrie and Anna. "Just make sure she doesn't forget to come to the meeting, okay?"

Too bad Spence was the only one.

CHAPTER
Three

"I can't believe the fifth grade has never won," Anna said as she set her tray of pizza down on the lunch table.

"I know," Carrie replied. "Not once in *ten years*."

"Twelve," Theresa said, peeling the foil top off her yogurt. "ECS has been holding spring carnival for twelve years; this will be the thirteenth. So far the eighth grade has won six times, the seventh grade four, and the sixth grade twice. But the fifth grade—*never*."

Theresa's friends stared at her. She dipped her spoon in and stirred.

"Thank you, Encyclopedia Allen," Anna said.

"Seriously," Carrie added with a giggle. "When did you become such an expert on spring carnival?" Carrie unwrapped her turkey sandwich and took a giant bite.

"Five minutes ago," Theresa said. "I stopped and checked the trophy cases next to the office on my way down here."

Anna squinted. "There are *trophies* for spring carnival?"

"Plaques, actually," Theresa said. "The class that comes up with the best theme and has the best booths gets a plaque with their class picture and year on it. And they get their picture in the paper, too. It's a pretty big deal."

"Not to me," Carrie said. "I mean, winning the plaque is cool and everything, but what I really want is the ice cream party."

"There's an ice cream party?" Anna asked. She opened her eyes so wide that both Carrie and Theresa had to laugh.

"I keep forgetting you're new here," Theresa said. She and Anna and Carrie had become so close that it was hard to believe Anna had only lived in Newcastle for six weeks. It seemed like the three of them had always been best friends.

"Yeah—there's an ice cream party," Theresa continued, "but it's not just *any* ice cream party. It's the *biggest* ice cream party *ever*."

Carrie nodded. "Ed's Soda Shop brings in something like thirty-two flavors along with tons of toppings—sprinkles, dips, candies, those little crunchy cookie things, hot fudge, caramel, whipped cream, cherries—just about everything you can think of."

"And you don't get tiny scoops, either," Theresa said. "Everyone fills huge bowls, and you can go back as many times as you want."

"Wow," Anna said. "That sounds awesome."

"My sister won when she was in seventh grade," Carrie added. "Lynn said it was like going into an ice cream parlor and taking whatever you wanted without having to pay."

The three girls sighed. Ed's Soda Shop had become their favorite after-school hangout, and the thought of having tons of ice cream—with all the trimmings—delivered to them for free was like a dream.

"We *have* to win," Carrie said.

"Definitely," Anna agreed.

"Double definitely," Theresa said. "We have to win that ice cream *and* end the fifth-grade losing streak." *And prove to my sister—and everyone else—that I can be involved in something without messing it up,* Theresa thought.

"Yeah," Carrie agreed. "But first we need to come up with a really good theme."

A slow smile crept onto Theresa's face. "I have an idea."

"You do?" Carrie and Anna asked at the same time.

Theresa nodded. "Mm-hm. I've been thinking about it all morning," she said, and she *had* been—ever since Amy had told her the fifth grade had no shot at winning. *We'll see who's laughing when I'm demolishing my second banana split,* Theresa thought.

"So?" Anna asked. "What's your theme?" She pulled an olive off the top of her pizza and popped it in her mouth.

"Okay," Theresa said. "I was thinking the theme should be—"

"Hollywood," Sharon Ross said, taking the seat next to Carrie's. "It's going to be Hollywood." She unwrapped a pat of butter and began mashing it into her potatoes while Theresa, Anna, and Carrie exchanged a bewildered look.

"Hollywood?" Anna asked.

"Yeah. You were talking about spring carnival, weren't you?"

"Well . . . yes," Theresa started, "but—"

"Then if you want to win, you should listen to me. My aunt is an interior decorator, and I have all kinds of ideas that will make the fifth-grade section the best."

Theresa rolled her eyes. Sharon was always

butting into things and taking over. And usually, because she was sort of a class leader, people just let her. Or at least they always had, until Anna had arrived.

"I'm sure your ideas are great, Sharon," Anna said with a twinge of condescension that made Theresa smirk. "But first we all have to agree on a theme."

"A theme? You mean for spring carnival?" Matt asked. He and Spence had arrived at the lunch table together, along with a few other fifth-grade boys, and plunked their trays down right in the middle opposite one another.

"Yo, ladies," Spence said. "Tell me you're going to win us that ice cream party."

"Hey—how did you know about the ice cream party?" Anna demanded. "You're newer here than I am."

"My man Matt filled me in," Spence said, grinning. "And when there's ice cream to be eaten, M. C. Spence will not be beaten. So . . . do we have a theme yet?"

Theresa perked up. This was her chance to show *everyone* just how creative she could be. Then maybe they'd all stop thinking of her as the forgetful, disorderly one. "Well, I was thinking we could do—"

"Hollywood," Sharon cut in for the second time. "I said it's going to be Hollywood." She gave Theresa a smug smile, then shoved a forkful of mashed potatoes into her mouth.

"That sounds cool," Kimberly Price said as she took the seat across from Sharon. Of course, Kimberly thought everything Sharon said was cool. If Sharon had suggested that they all go drink from a mud puddle, Kimberly would have been the first one outside with a straw.

"Hollywood, huh? What would we do for booths?" Matt asked.

"Tons of things," Sharon said. She set down her fork and leaned forward. "We could have dress-up booths and glamour photos. We could give out Oscars and Emmys. People could make their hand- or footprints in clay, just like they do when they give people stars outside Grauman's Chinese Theatre. We could have a karaoke machine and we could film people singing to make music videos. There could be celebrity look-alike contests, people could have their pictures printed out to look like they were on magazine covers . . . lots of stuff."

Theresa glanced around the table. Kimberly was nodding enthusiastically—of course—and Spence and Matt were kind of squinting, like they were trying to picture it all. Carrie and Anna just kind of shrugged when Theresa looked their way, and the other kids who had sat down while Sharon was talking seemed to be only half listening. No one seemed to think Hollywood was a bad idea, but no one seemed to be super-impressed by it, either.

Theresa ran her thumb and forefinger along the slender silver chain of her charm bracelet. She touched the angel and the unicorn that had supposedly brought Anna and Carrie good luck and wished for a little good luck of her own.

Then she took a deep breath and cleared her throat. "That sounds really interesting and everything," Theresa said, "and you have a lot of great ideas, Sharon, like Anna said, but . . . I have another suggestion."

"What's wrong with Hollywood?" Sharon demanded.

"Nothing," Theresa replied. "Except, well— didn't the eighth grade do something like that last year?"

"So?" Sharon said, cocking her head.

"*Soooo* . . . I just thought maybe we should try to do something original. Something that hasn't been done before," Theresa replied.

Carrie nodded. "Now that I think about it,

I'm pretty sure my sister's class did some kind of Hollywood theme one time, too. And it wasn't the year that they won."

"Sounds like that theme's been played out," Spence said.

Sharon sat up straight and narrowed her eyes. "Just because other classes have done it doesn't mean that we can't. We just have to do it better than they did."

"True enough," Spence said, and for a moment Sharon beamed triumphantly. "But," Spence continued, "we should cheer. / The original idea / is nothing to fear."

Sharon's smile turned into a scowl. "Do you always have to rhyme?"

"Only part-time," Spence replied with a grin. Matt chuckled, and the others did as well, but Sharon didn't look amused.

"So what's your idea, Theresa?" Matt asked, ignoring the glare Sharon was giving him.

"Oh—uh . . ." Theresa looked around. Suddenly everyone at the table was listening to her.

"Yeah, what is it?" Sharon snapped.

"Well, it's . . ." Theresa rubbed her lucky bracelet and cleared her throat. It was now or never. "I was thinking we could do . . . *three thousand four*."

There was silence at the table. Everyone stopped eating and stared blankly at Theresa.

"Three thousand and four *what?*" Sharon asked finally, tilting her head down and raising her eyebrows.

"No." Theresa shook her head. "Not three thousand and four *of* something. Three thousand four—*the year*," she explained. "You know, like a thousand years from now?"

"Ohhh," Carrie said. "I get it. So all our booths would have to be kind of . . . *futuristic*, right?"

"Right," Theresa said, feeling a bit more relaxed now that she'd gotten the words out. "We could call it 'Welcome to 3004' or '3004: A Space Odyssey' or something like that."

It was quiet for another minute, and Theresa chewed on the inside of her cheek as she waited for reactions. Then finally Spence nodded. "That's cool," he said. "I like it."

"Yeah," Matt agreed. "Me too."

Theresa's stomach fluttered with excitement. "Really?"

"Definitely," Anna said. "That's a neat idea."

Sharon clicked her tongue. "But what would we do for booths?" she demanded.

"There are lots of things we could do," Theresa said. "We could have a booth that showed what kind of clothes people will wear in the future. It could be a dress-up booth, like you were saying, or maybe just one of those wooden cutout things that you stand behind and have your picture taken. You know—so it looks like your head is on whatever body is in the picture?"

"I love those," Carrie said. "My dad and I had our picture taken like that once. I was a fisherman and he was a mermaid—it looked really funny. And I might even have a Polaroid camera we can use. I'm pretty sure my uncle has one."

"Great," Theresa said.

"Hey, since it's supposed to be the future, we could serve fortune cookies with funny predictions, like . . ." Anna squinted as she thought it over. Then suddenly her eyes lit up. "Like— 'In 3004 your great-great-great-great-great-great-great-granddaughter will be president of the earth.'"

"Or, 'In 3004 McDonald's will serve thirty million people . . . *on Mars*,'" Kimberly added with a smile. Sharon shot her a glare.

"Yo, we could do something about music in the future, too," Spence said.

"We could call it 'moon rock,'" Kimberly suggested, and again everyone laughed—except Sharon.

"I still think Hollywood would be better," she said. "Matt—you could do something on famous athletes."

Matt nodded thoughtfully, and then his face lit up. "I wonder what kind of extreme sports you could do in zero gravity," he said.

Sharon groaned.

"Hey—we could do something on food, too," Carrie added. "I'm sure people in 3004 would eat way differently than we do now."

"Right." Anna nodded. "And we can—"

"Okay—wait a second," Sharon jumped in. "You guys are all talking like we've already chosen this as our theme. Don't forget, we're having a class meeting next period to vote on ideas, and people might choose Hollywood."

As she looked around the table, Theresa noticed that just about everyone was avoiding eye contact with Sharon. It seemed pretty clear that none of them were considering voting for her idea. Then again, there were something like seventy-five fifth graders altogether, and Theresa was only sitting with six of them.

"That's true," Theresa said. "We don't really know what the theme is going to be yet."

Spence shrugged. "I like the future thing, man. There's so much we could do with it." He picked a french fry off his tray and started waving it around for emphasis. "Crazy space vehicles, life on other planets, intergalactic hip-hop . . ."

"Bungee jumping off space stations," Matt added. "I like the future thing, too—it's awesome."

"And no one's ever done it before," Theresa added.

Sharon frowned. "You don't know that," she scoffed.

"Yes, I do," Theresa replied. "The plaques in the trophy cases name all of the themes people have done, and no one's ever done anything about the future."

"So we could be the first," Anna said. "What was it you said about original ideas, Spence?"

"I said, 'The original idea is nothing to fear—'"

"Okay, okay—we've got it," Sharon snapped, and the table went silent.

"You know, Sharon," Theresa said after a moment, "if we did 3004, you could always do a booth on Hollywood and entertainment of the future."

Sharon tilted her head and sighed. "Yeah . . . I guess I could," she said.

Theresa grinned at Anna and Carrie, who smiled back at her. As obnoxious as Sharon could be at times, she made a good ally. She was loud and convincing, and people generally listened to her. So if Theresa could get her to go for the future theme, too, there was a good chance that it would get chosen.

"In fact, we could use a lot of my ideas for the future theme," Sharon went on. "And actually, now that I think about it, I guess which theme we choose isn't really all that important. It's what we do with it that matters. And with me in charge of decorating, we're sure to win."

Theresa's eyebrows shot up. *Sharon in charge?* Theresa had kind of been hoping that she would have the chance to see her idea all the way through. After all, she'd been the one to come up with it. And it would be the perfect opportunity for her to prove that she wasn't the ditz everyone seemed to think she was.

Again she stroked her lucky bracelet. "I was kind of thinking that maybe *I* could be in charge of the decorating—you know, if my theme gets chosen."

Sharon didn't even try to hide her laughter. "You've got to be kidding," she said, holding one hand across her stomach. "You? In charge of something that big?"

"What's wrong with that?" Theresa asked.

She glanced at her friends, but they had suddenly become captivated by the contents of their lunch trays.

"Oh, nothing," Sharon said. "Except for the fact that you're one of the least organized people I've ever met. You're always dropping things and forgetting things and tripping over things. I'm not trying to be mean or anything, but do you honestly think you could organize the entire fifth-grade area without messing something up?"

"I—" Theresa began, but just then the bell rang, signaling the end of lunch. Startled, Theresa jumped, bumping her tray slightly and sending her half-eaten cherry yogurt tumbling to the floor. "Oh, no," she moaned. There was pink goop all over.

"See what I mean?" Sharon said with a smirk. Then she picked up her tray and left. "See you at the class meeting."

Carrie and Anna rushed to Theresa's side with handfuls of napkins to help her clean up the mess.

"Don't listen to her," Anna said.

"She's just jealous that everyone liked your idea better than hers," Carrie added.

"Thanks," Theresa mumbled, but she couldn't

help wondering if they were being honest with her.

Neither Carrie nor Anna had said a word in her defense—or even looked up from their french fries—when Sharon had been going on and on about what a mess Theresa was. And if her two best friends didn't have faith in her ability to organize the decorations for spring carnival, what were the chances that anyone else would?

CHAPTER
Four

"All right, everyone. Let's get started," Mrs. Wessex called to the buzzing mass of students.

For the fifth-grade meeting, she and Mr. Kane had opened the divider between their rooms, and Mrs. McGuire, the other fifth-grade teacher, had brought her class in, too.

"As you well know," Mrs. Wessex began, "spring carnival is just around the corner, and we need to come up with a theme for our area."

Immediately everyone started whispering excitedly. Things like: "Have you heard about the ice cream party?" and, "We have to win!" There was so much energy in the room, it was hard to sit still.

"Quiet down, please," Mrs. Wessex called. "We need ideas for themes, and I can't hear you if everyone is talking at once. Go ahead and raise your hand if you have a suggestion."

A bunch of hands shot up in the air, and everyone started looking around to see who else was raising theirs.

"Go ahead," Anna said, nudging Theresa with her elbow. "Raise your hand. Tell her your theme."

"Ow," Theresa hissed. "Okay, okay." She was about to put her hand in the air when she saw Sharon's arm shoot up. She waved her arm around. "I have an idea, Mrs. Wessex," she said.

"All right, Sharon," Mrs. Wessex said. "What is it?"

Sharon stood and cleared her throat. "I thought we could do a future theme," she said. "Something like, 'Welcome to 3004' or '3004: A Space Odyssey.'"

Theresa's jaw dropped. She felt her friends' eyes on her, but she couldn't look away from Sharon. Meanwhile, the other students began to whisper their reactions. All the other students who had been raising their hands to say their ideas lowered them back to their sides. No one wanted to compete with what Sharon had just said. "Wow!" Theresa heard, and, "That would be awesome!" A lot of people seemed to really like her idea. Too bad Sharon was getting all the credit.

"That's a wonderful idea, Sharon," Mrs.

Wessex said, turning to write *3004* on the chalk-board. "Anyone else?"

"Um, Mrs. Wessex?" Anna piped up, her hand raised high.

"Yes, Anna?"

"I just wanted to let you know that the future theme was actually Theresa's idea—not Sharon's."

Eyes popped all around the room, and the whispering rose in volume as everyone darted looks at Sharon, Anna, Theresa, and Mrs. Wessex in turn.

"Okay, class—quiet down," Mrs. Wessex said. Meanwhile, Mr. Kane and Mrs. McGuire moved around the room, instructing individuals who were still talking to focus their attention up front.

"Sharon," Mrs. Wessex said when everyone had quieted down again. "Is that true? Was 3004 Theresa's idea?"

Sharon smiled and nodded as though she'd done absolutely nothing wrong. "Oh, yes," she said. "It was Theresa's idea. But she was so nervous about saying it in front of everybody that I thought I'd do it for her."

"Yeah, right," Theresa muttered out of the corner of her mouth.

Mrs. Wessex glanced toward Theresa briefly and pursed her lips. "I see," she said, and

Theresa had a feeling that she really did. "Well, thank you, Sharon, for getting the idea out there, and thank you, Theresa, for coming up with it. Now . . . do we have any others?"

The room was silent for a moment. Then Billy Rafuse raised his hand.

"William?" Mrs. Wessex called.

"I was just thinking, along with the 3004 thing, do you think we could do something on spaceships?"

"Oh, well," Mrs. Wessex said. "Yes—I'm sure we could, but we haven't actually chosen 3004 as our theme yet. That's just one of the suggestions."

"It would be so perfect, though," Billy insisted. "I have this huge NASA book at home, and I could design a bunch of rocket ships that could be cars of the future—"

"Hey—there's a Web site with cars of the future on it," Jeremy Gray cut in. "Maybe we could use some of those to—"

"My brother uses this 'search for extraterrestrials' program as a screen saver on his computer," Maria Mancini added. "Maybe we could set that up somewhere." One hand after another shot into the air as people came up with more ideas for the future theme. Pretty soon everyone was talking at once.

Theresa's face lit up as she listened. Kimberly was saying something about having a future fashion show, while Lauren Graham was suggesting a scale model of a 3004 space station. Spence and Matt were talking extreme sports and hip-hop again, and Adam Kersnowski thought it would be cool to have *The Jetsons* and *Futurama* playing on a TV somewhere.

"Wow—everyone really loves your idea, Resa," Carrie said.

Theresa grinned. "Seems like it," she agreed. "Thanks for speaking up for me, Anna."

"No problem," Anna replied. "I wasn't about to let Sharon steal your glory."

Just then Mrs. Wessex raised her hands. "All right, all right," she said. "I can see you're all very excited about Theresa's idea, and that's wonderful. But we only have a few minutes left to finish our class meeting, and I want to make sure we get everyone's ideas for themes on the board so we can take a vote."

Once again the class quieted down, and Mrs. Wessex repeated her original question. "Now—does anyone else have a *theme* suggestion?"

Theresa glanced around the room and waited, but no hands were raised.

"Nobody?" Mrs. Wessex asked, her brow furrowed.

She waited another fifteen seconds, but no one responded. "All right," she said slowly. "Well, then, let me just take an informal poll. How many of you—by a show of hands—would like to go with Theresa Allen's suggestion: 3004?"

Theresa was shocked to see nearly every hand in the room shoot up. Gradually she raised her hand, too, and in another five seconds she couldn't spot anyone who hadn't.

"Oh, my," Mrs. Wessex exclaimed, smiling. "I've never had a class reach consensus that quickly. Maybe it's a sign that this is the fifth grade's year to win."

"Yeah!" a few students called out. Then, when Mrs. Wessex turned to the board and circled Theresa's theme, everyone cheered.

"Now," Mrs. Wessex said, her voice rising over the chatter, "we're going to need someone to be in charge of coordinating all of the booths and overseeing the decorations for the area so that everything fits with the theme."

Theresa's heart fluttered. She wanted to be in charge more than anything! Planning and coordinating the decorations sounded like so much fun. If only she weren't so disorganized. Then maybe people would believe that she could do it. Maybe *she'd* even believe that she could do it.

"I'll be in charge of decorations, Mrs. Wessex," Sharon called out.

"Oh, that's very generous of you, Sharon," Mrs. Wessex said, "but I thought that since the theme was Theresa's idea, we'd see if she was interested in the position first. Theresa?"

Theresa's stomach flipped. Everyone in the room was staring at her. Maria and Lauren were whispering and giggling over in the corner, and Theresa was positive they were talking about her and what a joke it would be for her to be in charge.

"Oh . . . uh," Theresa stuttered. She hadn't expected Mrs. Wessex to just offer her the position. She'd assumed the class would have to vote for a decorating chairperson, and it seemed clear from all of the shocked expressions around her that she wouldn't have been their first choice.

"Theresa?" Mrs. Wessex repeated. "What do you think?"

"Well . . ." Theresa hesitated. "I . . ." She glanced around. Carrie and Anna were staring at her wide-eyed, and Sharon was scowling. Not exactly votes of confidence.

"Theresa?" Mrs. Wessex asked again.

Theresa swallowed hard. She wanted to, but she wasn't sure she should. Or, more accurately, she wasn't sure she *could*. Then she heard her sister's voice—"*You'd lose your feet if they weren't attached to your ankles.*" Suddenly a feeling of indignation rose in her chest.

"I'll do it!" Theresa said suddenly. The words came out a little louder than she had meant them to, but at least they were out there.

"Wonderful," Mrs. Wessex said, beaming at Theresa. "I'm sure you'll do an excellent job."

Theresa smiled nervously. She certainly hoped she would, but part of her was already wondering if she'd made the right decision. Apparently her friends were wondering the same thing—Anna and Carrie were both staring at her cautiously.

"Are you sure you want to do this, Resa?" Carrie whispered. "That's a lot of . . . *work.*"

"And a lot of organizing, too," Anna piped in.

Oh, great, Theresa thought. Her friends didn't think she could do it. A sudden wave of anxiety washed over her, and she felt her palms begin to sweat. Maybe they were right. Being in charge of the entire fifth-grade area wasn't going to be easy, and being organized wasn't exactly Theresa's strong point.

Maybe I should let somebody else do it, Theresa thought. She was just about to raise her hand and bow out when Mrs. Wessex began talking again.

"All right, so that's settled. Tonight I want everyone to think about booth ideas to go along with Theresa's theme. We'll be having another class meeting tomorrow during third period to iron out all of the details. And then, once your booths have been approved, you can start working on them. Theresa, you can focus on coming up with some general decorating ideas for now, and then when we know what all of the booths are going to be, I'll get you a copy of the list so that you can check in with everyone and make sure everything gets coordinated. Okay?"

"Okay," Theresa said. *What have I gotten myself into?* she thought. What if she couldn't handle it? What if she let the whole class down and blew their chance to be the first fifth grade to win spring carnival? She pressed her eyes closed and heard Sharon's words echoing in her head. "*You've got to be kidding! You? In charge of something that big?*" And then in the distance she heard Sharon's voice again—but this time it was for real.

She was all the way across the room in a group with Billy, Jeremy, Maria, and Lauren, and she was talking softly, but Theresa could still hear her. It was like her ears had focused in on the conversation the minute she'd heard Sharon say her name.

"I can't believe Mrs. Wessex put *Theresa* in charge," she was saying. "She is so totally klutzy and disorganized. There goes our shot at winning." Theresa tried to keep listening, but she was distracted by Carrie tugging at her arm.

"Resa—come on. We have to get to science class," she said.

"Huh? Oh, right," Theresa said, gathering up her books. She wished she'd been able to hear whether or not the others agreed with Sharon, but it was too late now. Everyone was filtering out of the room to get to their fifth-period class.

"Shoot," Theresa mumbled. It would have been nice to know how the others had responded.

"Theresa—is something wrong?" Anna asked.

"Oh, no. It's nothing," Theresa fibbed. She didn't want to repeat what she'd overheard—it would only make them feel bad for her, and it would make her feel worse. Besides, what if they agreed with Sharon?

"Good," Anna said. "Then let's go."

As they walked into the hallway, Carrie turned to face the other two girls. "Hey—how did you guys do on that homework, anyway?"

"What homework?" Theresa asked.

"You know, the reading we had to do for science class, with all those questions about solar power and light waves. I was totally lost by the end of the chapter," Carrie said.

"Wait a second—we had science homework last night?" Theresa said. "When did Mr. Howell assign that?"

"Yesterday during class," Anna said. "He wrote it on the side of the chalkboard like he always does."

"Oh, man," Theresa said. "He's going to kill me. I totally spaced out. Sometimes I'm so—" Theresa stopped short, but she was all too aware of the word she'd been about to use: *disorganized*.

Jeez. If she couldn't even stay on top of her homework assignments, how was she going to keep up with all of this spring carnival stuff? Something told her she'd bitten off way more than she could chew. And when all was said and done, Amy would know she'd been right. With Theresa involved, the fifth grade didn't stand a chance.

CHAPTER
Five

"Theresa—your ice cream is starting to drip," Carrie said. "Either you have to hold it yourself, or I'm going to start licking it."

"Okay, okay. Just a second," Theresa said. "I want to show you what I got at Sara's." She opened the white plastic bag she was holding and removed what looked like a black, leatherbound book. "Ta-da!" she said, setting it on the large, round, green metal table in the middle of the mall's food court.

"What's that?" Anna asked, taking a bite of mint chocolate chip.

"My new planner," Theresa announced. She held the book at several different angles and ran her hand across the cover like a game show model.

"Beautiful," Carrie said. "Now take your ice cream."

"Fine," Theresa replied. She took the cone from Carrie's hand and began licking the nearly melted coffee ice cream all around the edges. In less than fifteen seconds she had all the drips stopped and everything under control. "There," she said. "Now—don't you want to know why I bought myself a planner?"

"Is this a trick question?" Anna asked. "Because I sort of figured it had something to do with the way Mr. Howell said, 'Theresa—you need to get a planner,' in science class today." Carrie giggled and Theresa cocked her head.

"Very funny," she said. "But that's only part of the reason." She unsnapped a clasp on the front of the planner and flipped it open. "See— it has a calendar section in the front with plenty of space for me to write all my assignments, but it also has all this other stuff."

Theresa waved her hand over the back section of the planner, which was full of different sorts of paper—lined, blank, graph, and colored.

"Maybe you should drop out of school and make a career out of modeling planners on the Home Shopping Network," Anna suggested.

"*Anna,*" Theresa groaned.

Carrie pointed to Theresa's cone. "You're dripping," she said, but her warning came too late. A dark brown chocolate chip covered in light brown coffee ice cream splattered onto the paper in Theresa's planner.

"Shoot!" Theresa reached for a napkin. She dabbed at the ice cream, but while she was wiping it, more ice cream fell off her cone and landed on the paper. By the time she was done, sticky brown drips covered the back section, causing most of the pages to stick together. Theresa stared at it. "I can't believe I just did that."

"At least the calendar part is still okay," Carrie said, wincing slightly.

"Yeah." Theresa snorted. "I guess."

Anna jogged over to Ed's, where the girls had gotten their ice cream, and returned with a handful of napkins, a bowl, and a plastic spoon. "Here," she said. "Just stick your ice cream in the bowl, and then show us the rest of your stuff."

Theresa sighed. "Thanks, Anna," she said. She upended her cone and plunged it into the bowl, ice cream first. Then, after wiping her hands clean on a few napkins, she examined her planner.

"Well, a few pages are still okay," she said. "But not enough to help me keep track of everything for spring carnival." Theresa shook her head and exhaled heavily. "Maybe Sharon was right. Maybe I should tell Mrs. Wessex to choose someone else to be in charge."

"Well . . ." Anna tilted her head. "If you're not comfortable being in charge, you could always just tell her you've changed your mind."

"I didn't say I was *uncomfortable*," Theresa said. "I mean, I *want* to do it—I just don't want to mess everything up."

"I'm sure you won't," Carrie said, but Theresa couldn't help feeling that she didn't sound all that convinced.

"Did you get anything else at Sara's?" Anna asked, pointing to Theresa's bag. "It looks like something else is in there."

"Oh," Theresa said, picking up the white plastic bag on her lap. "Yeah, there is, but—"

"Well, show it to us," Anna said.

Theresa sighed again. It seemed kind of pointless now that her planner was virtually destroyed. She reached into the bag and pulled out a long black tube with white caps at each end.

"Uh, Theresa," Anna started. "Is that a magic wand?"

"I wish," Theresa said. She waved it around a few times and said, "Abracadabra! Fix my planner! Hocus-pocus! Finish my science homework!"

"That would be awesome," Carrie said. "I'd

use it to make myself an endless supply of black raspberry ice cream."

"No way—mint chocolate chip," Anna said. "But you said it wasn't a magic wand. So . . . what is it?"

Theresa popped a white cap off one end and tilted the tube until a pen slid out. It was shiny and black, just like the tube, except that it had glittery silver stars and moons all over it. Perched at the top was a silver fairy with delicate wire mesh wings and a wand with a star on the end.

"Wow, that's really pretty, Resa," Carrie said.

"Thanks," Theresa said. "I was going to keep it with my planner. See—there's a little pen holder on the side." She slid the pen into a small elastic loop, then drew her hand back quickly. "Ew!" she said, wiping ice cream off her hand. Apparently she'd missed a spot when she was cleaning up. "Great, now my pen's all sticky, too."

"I'm sure you can wash it off," Anna said.

"Yeah, maybe," Theresa said. But she was feeling pretty discouraged. It seemed like the harder she tried to get organized, the worse things got.

"Yo—ladies," a familiar voice called. Theresa looked up to see Spence and Matt approaching the table. Each of the boys pulled out a chair, flipped it around, and sat down straddling the back of it. "What's going down?"

"My self-esteem," Theresa mumbled.

"What was that?" Spence asked.

Theresa shook her head. "Nothing," she said. "I'm just trying to get organized for spring carnival, and it's not going so well."

"Oh, that's right," Matt said, turning to Theresa. "You're in charge of everything, aren't you? That's great that everyone went for your idea."

Theresa looked down at her ruined planner. "I just hope I don't screw it up."

"You won't," Spence said. "The decorations will be ill / but right now it's time to chill. / You girls up for some danger? / A game of Storm Ranger?"

Theresa smiled in spite of herself. "How do you do that?" she asked.

Spence widened his eyes. "Do what?"

"Rhyme everything."

"Oh, that," Spence said. "I don't know. It just kind of happens—I open my mouth and start rappin'. It's probably from listening to so much hip-hop, you know? It's like reading a lot of Dr. Seuss. / Pretty soon your tongue gets loose."

"And you start to sound like Mother Goose," Carrie said.

"Not bad, not bad," Spence said, giving

Carrie a high five. "We'll have you freestyling in no time."

"I don't know about that," Carrie said, "but I would like to try Storm Ranger. I've heard Anna and Matt talk about it so much, I feel like I already know how to play."

"All right," Spence said. "Anyone else?"

"Anna will play," Matt said. "She has to try to beat my latest high score. I made it to level twelve yesterday and saw a completely new enemy."

"You did?" Anna said. "Who was it?"

"Mr. Feetstink," Matt said with a perfectly straight face.

"Mr. Feetstink?" Theresa repeated. "Who's he?"

"He's supposed to be a high school gym teacher who mutated when Dr. Sphere hit him with his chaos laser," Matt explained. "Now he has forty-two feet and he attacks by taking off his sneakers and blasting you with his foot odor."

"That's great," Spence said, chuckling. "I *have* to play this game. Anna, Theresa—you in?"

"I am," Anna said.

"Ohhh," Theresa said. "I'd like to, but . . ." She stared down at her sticky planner and her even stickier pen. "I can't." She shook her head. "I have to figure out some of this spring carnival stuff."

"Do you want us to stay and help?" Carrie asked.

"No—you guys go ahead without me," Theresa said.

"Are you sure?" Anna asked.

"Definitely," Theresa replied. "Have a good time—and shatter Matt's high score."

Anna laughed. "I will," she said. "And then I'll show Carrie how to do it, too."

"Oh, right," Matt said. "Like it's that easy."

"It is for me," Anna said with a shrug.

Theresa smiled as she watched them walk toward the arcade, Anna and Matt trading insults all the way. Once they were out of sight, she looked down at the table and focused on her planner. "Time to get to work," she told herself.

She grabbed her fairy pen and gave it a tug, but thanks to the ice cream spill, it was stuck in its holder. "Ugh," Theresa groaned. She gave it another tug, but it still wouldn't come loose. Frustrated, Theresa tightened her grip around the fairy and gave it one more pull—too hard a pull, as it turned out.

The pen came free right away, but Theresa had pulled so forcefully that she'd ended up pulling the fairy right off the end. "Oh, no," Theresa said. "I can't believe I just broke it! I've only owned it for ten minutes!"

She set the fairy ornament on the table and

looked at it closely. "If there ever was a sign, this is it. I should just tell Mrs. Wessex I've changed my mind. If I can't even *touch* organizing materials without messing them up, then I certainly can't do the organizing!" She reached for the small silver ornament on the table, intending to toss it in the garbage along with her now-ruined planner. But just as she was about to grab it, it moved.

Theresa gasped.

First it just sort of wobbled to the right. Then it shifted back to the left. And then, while Theresa watched, wide-eyed, the tiny fairy began to grow. Slowly at first, then faster, until she was nearly two inches tall. Her wings and wand vanished, and her silver coloring melted away.

Instead, the little sprite was wearing a white T-shirt, brown cargo shorts, a Red Sox baseball cap, and a backpack. She had thick wool socks and muddy hiking boots, and in one hand she was holding a long, thick stick that reached all the way to the ground.

"I'm ready when you—" the fairy started. Then she blinked a few times and looked around. "Wait a second," she said. "This is *not* the Missouri River, and you're *definitely* not Sacajawea."

CHAPTER
Six

"Wh-Who . . . w-what?" stammered Theresa. She had to be seeing things.

"I hate it when this happens." The little fairy shook her head. She stuffed her hand into her front pocket and dug around frantically for something. "Oh, no—don't tell me I left it at home."

Left what at home? Theresa wondered. She was too stunned to say it out loud.

Suddenly the tiny sprite clutched something in her hand and exhaled. "Phew," she said, extracting a small purple stone from her pocket. "Amethyst," she said to Theresa. "My lucky gem. It calms me—helps me to focus. If you'll just excuse me for a moment."

The little fairy turned around and hopped into the air. The next thing Theresa knew, she was hovering about a foot above the table, sitting cross-legged on a purple pillow with yellow tassels at the corners.

"What are you—?"

"Shhh," the fairy murmured. "I'm meditating."

She placed the amethyst on the pillow in front of her, closed her eyes, and rested her hands on her knees, palms up. "Deep breath in," she said to herself, "and a deep breath out. Another deep breath in. And a deep breath out. Okay—one more time. Deep breath in and a deep breath out." She sat silently for a moment, then scooped up the amethyst and snapped her fingers.

"Ahhh, that's better," she said. "I feel much more centered now. Okay—where were we?"

Theresa stared and blinked. "I think you said something about Sacajawea," she offered.

"Oh, that's right," the fairy said. "I was just about to hike out of the Missouri River Valley with Lewis and Clark when I got sent here. Oh, well. I guess I'll have to finish that trail another day."

"You were hiking with *Lewis and Clark*? And *Sacajawea*?"

"Yes. Lovely people, all of them. And so brave. I—"

Just then a high-pitched beeping came from out of nowhere. "Oh—that's me," the fairy said. She unclipped a small black pager from her shorts. "Time to find out what this is all about. I'll just be a moment, okay?"

"Uh . . . okay," Theresa replied. She watched as the fairy tossed the pager into the air and snapped her fingers. Instantly the pager was transformed into what looked like a miniature hovering computer screen.

Theresa could see that it was covered with words, but the letters were far too small for her to read. The fairy, however, was having no trouble. She kept pointing at the screen and waving her finger, scrolling through documents and muttering to herself every now and then.

"Mm-hm. . . mm-hm . . . Theresa Allen . . . right . . . *ohhh—klutzy and disorganized?* That wasn't very nice. Mm-hm . . . right, I see . . . spring carnival . . . confidence issues . . . organizationally challenged . . . yep . . . okay . . . got it."

She snapped her fingers again, turning the monitor back into a tiny pager, which she caught in her hand and clipped back onto her shorts.

"Okay," she said. "Why don't you have a nice, soothing cup of chamomile tea and tell me all about this spring carnival event." The fairy circled one of her hands in the air, and a cup and saucer appeared in front of Theresa.

"Um, I don't drink tea," Theresa said.

"No problem," the fairy said. "What would you like? Cocoa? Apple juice? Water with lemon?" With each suggestion she pointed to the cup in front of Theresa, transforming its contents into the various beverages.

"Actually, I'm fine," Theresa said.

"Suit yourself," the fairy said. She pointed one last time and the cup disappeared altogether. Theresa leaned forward and rested her head on her hands so that she was only inches away from the tiny figure.

"Are you real?" she whispered. "Or am I dreaming?"

The fairy reached forward and jabbed Theresa's hand with her stick. "Ow!" Theresa said, jerking her hand back.

"I'm real. Dreams don't leave imprints," the fairy said. Theresa glanced at the spot where she'd been hit and saw a tiny red mark.

"No, I guess they don't," Theresa said. "But still—"

"I know," the fairy replied. "You've probably never seen a magical being before, but trust me— I *am* real. I'm Isadora, by the way. Izzy for short."

"I'm Theresa," Theresa said. "But then, I guess you knew that." The small figure smiled. "So then—are you really a *fairy*?"

Izzy nodded. "I certainly am—certified by the UFC."

"The *what*?"

"The UFC—Universal Fairy College. I have an undergraduate degree in general enchantment and a master's in social work."

"Wow," Theresa said. "But if you're a—" She glanced around to make sure no one was watching or listening to her. No one seemed to be, but she lowered her voice just in case. "If you're a fairy, why don't you have—?"

Izzy held up her hands. "Wings, right? You were going to say wings, weren't you?"

"Well, yeah," Theresa said. "And a magic wand."

The fairy shook her head, swishing her long brown ponytail back and forth. "I will never understand why you humans make us look so ridiculous."

"What do you mean?" Theresa said. "I think fairies are pretty."

"Pretty? Maybe. But foolish nonetheless. We're always drawn like cute little Barbie dolls flitting about in short skirts and butterfly wings. It's really not a very flattering image."

"You mean, fairies don't fly?" Theresa asked.

"Oh, we fly," Izzy said. "But we don't need

wings to do it. Of course, some fairies do wear wings from time to time, but only for special occasions. You know . . . weddings, graduations—things like that. But not all the time—and definitely not to fly. They'd get in the way."

"What about magic wands?" Theresa asked.

"Wands are for beginners," Izzy said. "I gave mine up during my second year of graduate school. Now I just wave my hands or snap my fingers or nod—whatever I feel like doing. It's all the same. See?"

Izzy stuck out her hand and clenched it into a fist, and across the table a napkin curled itself up into a ball. Then she flicked open her fingers and it went sailing into the trash.

"Cool," Theresa said, but the fairy wasn't done.

Next, Izzy snapped her fingers, and Theresa watched in amazement as her melted ice cream formed itself into a neat scoop again. Then, when Izzy raised her eyebrows and glanced at Theresa, the ice-cream cone righted itself and floated over to Theresa, who grabbed it and took a lick.

"Good as new, right?" Izzy said, smiling.

"Definitely," Theresa said.

Finally Isadora folded her arms at chest level and nodded, changing her entire outfit from shorts, T-shirt, hiking boots, and backpack into jeans, a peasant blouse, and Birkenstock sandals in the blink of an eye. Her Red Sox cap was gone, and her long brown hair hung loosely about her shoulders and cascaded down her back.

"Wow," Theresa said. "That's amazing."

"It comes in pretty handy," Isadora said.

"I bet," Theresa agreed.

"So—let's get down to business. Talk to me about spring carnival," Isadora said. "I'm here to help you out."

"You *are*?" Theresa exclaimed. "Awesome! So then can you just, like, snap your fingers and get everything organized for me?"

Izzy tilted her head and winced. "Unfortunately that's not the way it works."

"Why not?"

"Well, have you ever heard the expression 'Give a girl a fish and she'll eat for a day; teach a girl to fish and she'll eat for life'?"

"*No-o*," Theresa said. "What does fishing have to do with spring carnival?"

"Yo, Tee—that's a good question." Theresa spun around to see Spence standing behind her. "And here's another one—who are you talking to?"

CHAPTER
Seven

"Oh, I, uh," Theresa started. She glanced from Spence down to Izzy and back again.

"What'd you do—get another ice cream?" Spence asked, squinting at Theresa's perfectly intact cone.

"My other one, uh, melted." She stared down at Izzy again and saw that Spence had followed her gaze, but he didn't appear in the least bit shocked. If anything, he seemed puzzled as to what she was looking at. Evidently he couldn't see the tiny fairy standing there.

"Who's this?" Izzy asked.

"Spence," Theresa responded automatically.

"Yo," Spence replied. "I'm right here—you got my ear."

"Oh, right," Theresa said. If Spence couldn't see Izzy, he probably couldn't hear her, either, which meant that Theresa needed to stop answering her out loud. Unless, of course, she wanted Spence to think she was insane.

"Hey, you okay, Tee?" Spence asked. "You look a little . . . spooked."

Theresa gave a nervous laugh. "Spooked?" she said. "No, I just—well, you sort of scared me before. I was, you know, trying to come up with ideas for spring carnival, and I guess I was pretty focused."

"I'll say you were," Spence agreed. "You were talking to yourself."

"Oh, I do that sometimes," Theresa said quickly. "It's sort of a weird habit, I know."

"Ain't no thang," Spence said. "I talk to myself all the time."

"I like this boy," Izzy said. "He's very in touch with his inner self. And he has unique speech patterns."

Theresa had to fake a cough to keep herself from laughing.

"Where's everyone else?" Theresa asked when she had regained her composure.

"Still in the arcade," Spence said. "Carrie's on her third game with Anna coaching, and then Anna and Matt are gonna go head-to-head."

Theresa took a lick from her ice cream. "Did you play?" she asked.

"I got squashed on level five by some kind of lizard-horse-snake thing."

"Too bad," Theresa said.

"Nah, it's all right," Spence replied, pulling out a chair. "I wanted to come back and talk to you about spring carnival anyway."

Theresa raised her eyebrows. "You *did*?" she asked. She bit off a big section of chocolate cappuccino chunk and licked her lips.

"Yeah, I need help coming up with an idea for a booth."

"Ahhh," Izzy said, smiling at Theresa. "People seek you out for advice. You're a natural leader."

Theresa snorted. "The ideas come easy—it's the organization I'm worried about," she muttered.

"Whoa—can you play that back for me one time?" Spence said.

"Oh, sorry," Theresa replied, realizing she'd done it again. "I guess I was just thinking out loud." She turned away from Spence, pretending to wipe her chin with a napkin and mimed locking her mouth shut and throwing away the key to Izzy.

"I can be quiet," the little fairy said. She snapped her fingers and went back to hovering on her pillow again.

Theresa turned to Spence. "So," she said, having another bite of ice cream, "what did you have in mind?"

"Well, I wanted to do something hip-hop related."

"That's a shocker," Theresa joked. "Are you doing it with Matt?"

"Nah—Matt wants to do some kind of sports thing," Spence said. "I'm on my own right now, which is no problem. Trouble is, I'm not sure what to *do* for the booth other than maybe play music and call it intergalactic hip-hop, you know? I mean, how do I make it, like, a *booth*?"

"Mmm." Theresa nodded. "I see what you mean." She licked her ice cream while she thought it over. A couple of seconds later the idea came to her in a flash.

"How about this—you could call your booth something like 'Spence's Intergalactic Hip-Hop Stop' and have it be a club that plays music and serves trendy refreshments—with hip-hop names, of course. *Or*"—Theresa paused to lick her cone again—"you could make it into a futuristic music store, and you could pretend to be a big hip-hop star from another galaxy who's there for some kind of promotion. You could come up with a bunch of fake album covers, and people could try to compete with you at some kind of rapping or rhyming game."

"You mean like a freestyle battle?"

"I guess," Theresa said. "Is that what you'd call it?"

"Yep. Two MCs trading phrases, trying to outdo each other—that's a battle. Cool idea, Tee. Thanks."

"Sure," Theresa said, "but I didn't really do anything."

"But you did—you gave me a place to start. And you also made me hungry," Spence added, eyeing her ice-cream cone. "I'm gonna go score a scoop—you need anything?"

"No, I'm all set, thanks," Theresa said. As Spence jogged over to Ed's, she looked down at Izzy, who was giving her a smug smile.

"That was wonderful," Izzy said. "He came to you for help, and you solved his problem. You're very good at this."

Theresa rolled her eyes. "I told you—the ideas come easy to me. It's keeping organized that gives me trouble."

"Nonsense. You just have to stay focused and trust your instincts."

"My instincts ruined my planner," Theresa said, nodding at the sticky mess of pages in front of her.

"No problem," Izzy said. She waved both of her hands in wide circles, and, right before Theresa's eyes, the planner went from stained and gooey to perfectly clean.

"Whoa—thanks," Theresa said, lifting it into the air to examine it.

Suddenly the little fairy hopped down and started glancing around. "Is it me, or did it just get really cold in here?"

"Huh?"

"Theresa!" a familiar voice called.

"Ugh," Theresa groaned. "It's not you," she told Izzy. She turned around to see Sharon approaching while Kimberly, Lauren, and Maria stayed behind chatting in a small group.

"Hey," Sharon said, "we just saw Carrie, Matt, and Anna in the arcade, and they said you were down here working on spring carnival stuff."

"Ooh," Izzy said, narrowing her eyes. "I'm getting a really bad vibe from this one—lots of negative energy. Something tells me you shouldn't trust her."

"I don't," Theresa said. Then she looked up at Sharon. "I mean, I *am*," she corrected herself quickly. "Working on spring carnival stuff, that is." She glanced down at Izzy, and the fairy sighed.

"I know. Quiet," she said, jumping back onto her floating pillow.

"So, how's it going?" Sharon asked. "Have you come up with a lot of decorating ideas yet?"

"*Well* . . ." Theresa hesitated.

"You know," Sharon went on, "at first I was kind of upset that you got picked to be in charge of our theme instead of me, but now I'm kind of glad."

Theresa narrowed her eyes. "You are?" she asked.

"Absolutely," Sharon said. "I mean, you have *so* much work to do! You have to decide how to decorate our section of the gym and keep track of what everyone's planning to do for booths. You'll need to find out how much you can spend on decorations and submit some kind of budget to Mrs. Wessex. At some point you'll have to get together a decorating committee and find time to meet to plan things out, and then you'll have to be at school early to help set everything up and stay late to make sure it all gets taken down. Phew! That's a lot of work. But then, if you weren't up for it, I guess you wouldn't have told Mrs. Wessex you could do it."

"Wow, I don't usually dislike people," Izzy commented from her pillow, "but in her case, I might have to make an exception."

Theresa scratched her head and tried to ignore her little friend. "Um . . . what are you doing for a booth, Sharon?" she asked.

"I haven't decided yet," Sharon said. "I'm having a hard time coming up with something to fit your theme."

"*My* theme?" Theresa said.

"Well, of course—it was *your* idea, right? Isn't that what Anna said? '*The future theme was Theresa's idea, not Sharon's*?*'"

"Um—"

"Oh, it's okay," Sharon said. "I'm actually glad she cleared that up. I've heard a lot of people say they're having a hard time with the theme, and I'd hate for them to think it was my idea. I mean, 3004 sounded good during the class meeting and all, but no one really seems to be coming up with any good booth ideas. But then, I'm sure people will come to you if they have problems."

"Well," Theresa said, "Spence did." She nodded toward Ed's, where Spence was just paying for a huge cone with three different-colored scoops of ice cream on top.

"Hey, Sharon," Kimberly said, running up to her side. "Spence is over at Ed's. Lauren, Maria, and I are going to head over, 'kay?"

"Okay," Sharon said. "I'll meet you over there." Kimberly ran back to the others, and then the three of them headed toward Spence, giggling all the way. "They are *so* immature," Sharon remarked, shaking her head. "Well, anyway, good luck with everything. Oh—I see you bought a planner."

"I did," Theresa said. "I think it will really help."

Sharon shrugged. "Maybe," she said. "But my mother—she's a lawyer, you know—she says that I was born organized. It's in my genes."

"In your—?"

"Genes," Sharon said. "You know—I inherited my ability to stay organized from her. And my dad—he's really organized, too. My mom says people either have it or they don't, and that stuff like planners and PalmPilots may make a person *look* organized for a while, but they don't really help in the long run."

"Oh," Theresa said. "Well—"

"Anyway, I have to get going," Sharon interrupted. "But hey—don't worry about your theme. I don't think it's nearly as lame as everyone else seems to. And besides, I'm sure you'll get a chance to help everyone with their problems at tomorrow's class meeting."

"That's it," Theresa heard a small voice say, and when she looked up, Isadora was floating above Sharon's head, sitting cross-legged on a big gray storm cloud. "Say the word and I'll soak her," the fairy said.

"Izzy!" Theresa shouted.

Sharon drew back. "Huh?"

"Oh, uh . . ." Theresa glanced nervously at Sharon, who was staring at her like she'd gone completely insane. "It's just . . . I was saying . . ."

"'Is he,'" Sharon said. "You shouted out, 'Is he.'"

"Right," Theresa said. "I meant, um, Spence. I think he's done getting his ice cream. I was going to say, 'Is he leaving?' Because I thought you wanted to talk to him—didn't you?"

Sharon squinted at Theresa. "Not really," she said. "But I guess I should catch up with Kimberly and the others." She nodded toward Theresa's planner and smirked. "Good luck getting organized."

"Thanks," Theresa said, forcing herself to smile. But as soon as Sharon turned to walk away, she dropped her head into her hands and moaned.

Izzy snapped her fingers, vaporized the cloud, and glided down to the table, where she stood, rubbing her amethyst in her hands. "Whoa. I don't know what got into me there. I'm usually very calm, but that girl—"

"Sharon has a way of getting to people," Theresa said.

"I'll say," Izzy agreed. She plunked the amethyst into her front pocket and stood with her arms at her sides, her feet about a half-inch apart.

"Izzy?" Theresa said.

"Shhh!" hissed the fairy. Then she took a deep breath, raising both arms into the air and bringing her palms together above her head. Theresa watched as Isadora took a big step forward with her right leg. She sank into a deep lunge and held it—her arms straight, her palms pressed together, and her gaze focused straight ahead. After about thirty seconds she stepped back, bringing her legs together again, took another deep breath, and repeated the lunge position with her left leg forward.

Theresa watched and waited until finally, after another thirty seconds had passed, Izzy stepped back, lowered her arms, and exhaled heavily. "Phew. Warrior one is my favorite pose. It always centers me and brings me back to a place of peace."

Theresa squinted. *A place of peace?* This fairy

just kept getting weirder and weirder. No wings, no wand, and now . . . *yoga*?

"Ahhh, that's better," Izzy said, shaking out her arms and legs. "I feel much more relaxed now. How about you? Do you need a little centering exercise? I could lead you through a few stretches."

Theresa glanced at all the people milling about and wondered how it would look if she stood up and started practicing yoga in the middle of the food court. "Thanks, but I think I'll pass," she told Izzy.

"Suit yourself," Isadora said with a shrug. "Just as long as you didn't believe any of that stuff Sharon was saying about spring carnival."

Theresa winced.

"You didn't . . . *did you*?" Izzy asked.

"Maybe just a little," she said with a half shrug.

"You can't," Izzy told her. "She was *trying* to upset you. That's the whole reason she came over here. I hate people like that. I mean— shoot! There I go again." In one quick motion Isadora plunged herself back into warrior one. "*Hate* is a very strong word," she said, keeping her gaze forward. "I don't *hate* her. I just—" All at once the little fairy dropped her arms to her sides and shook her head.

"Are you okay, Izzy?" Theresa asked.

Isadora stared up at Theresa, shamefaced. "I have anger issues," she said quietly.

"Anger issues?" Theresa repeated.

Izzy nodded and glanced down at the table. "Like I said, I'm usually very calm, but every once in a while someone pushes my buttons—you know what I mean?"

Theresa gazed toward Ed's, where Sharon and the others were still standing. "I know what you mean."

"One time," Izzy continued, her head still lowered, "I turned a snobby rich woman into a miniature poodle for two whole days. I thought seeing life as a lapdog might humble her."

"You turned her into a—?" Theresa began. Then she giggled. "Did it work?"

"Well, *yes*," Isadora answered. "She definitely gained a little perspective. But the UFC didn't exactly approve. Fairies aren't supposed to change people into animals—at least not without an advanced degree in transmogrification."

"Oh," Theresa said. "I see."

"Still, I think that friend of yours deserved a little rainstorm. It might have cooled her down a bit," Izzy said.

"Yeah, maybe," Theresa agreed, "and it would have been kind of funny, too."

"Well, I'll try to control myself in the future, but if she starts talking like that again, I just might have to douse her," Izzy said.

Theresa pictured Sharon getting soaked by a shower in the middle of the mall and chuckled. But when she remembered all the things Sharon had said, her smile faded.

"Unfortunately, I think Sharon's right," Theresa said.

"Are you joking?" Izzy asked.

"No," Theresa replied, shaking her head. "I mean, the planner is a nice idea, but owning it isn't going to change the way I am. I'm horrible at keeping organized. I can't keep track of all the stuff she was talking about! Budgets, booth ideas, decorations, a committee—it's too much."

"It may sound like a lot when you lump it all together like that, but trust me—you can do it," Izzy said. "You just have to take it step by step."

"Izzy," Theresa said, "you don't understand. I'm a total mental klutz. I had already forgotten that there *was* a class meeting tomorrow! I can't stay on top of all of this. Planner or no planner, I'm just not good at being organized."

"Do you know how many negative statements you just made about yourself?" Izzy asked.

"Huh?"

"Seven," Isadora said. "At least. And that's too many. Come on—grab all of your stuff and let's get out of here. We've got work to do."

"Where are we going?" Theresa asked.

"Home," Izzy said. "There are too many distractions at the mall."

"All right," Theresa said with a sigh. She stood up and stuffed her planner and her broken pen back into the Sara's bag, put on her backpack, and offered her outstretched palm to Izzy.

Izzy glanced down at Theresa's hand. "What's that for?"

"Hop on," Theresa said. "I'll put you in my pocket or something."

"Oh, that's very kind of you, but no thanks," Izzy said. "Pocket travel gives me motion sickness. I'll meet you there." And with that, she raised both arms above her head dramatically and vanished, floating pillow and all.

I'll have to see if she can teach me that trick, Theresa thought. *That way, when everyone starts blaming me for the fifth grade's last-place finish at spring carnival, I can just disappear.*

CHAPTER
Eight

Theresa climbed the stairs to her room slowly. *Izzy better have some good ideas,* she thought, *or I'm doomed.*

Secretly, she was hoping the little fairy would just snap her fingers and produce lists of ideas and then wiggle her nose and turn Theresa into an organizational genius. But something about the whole "teach a girl to fish" quote told her it wasn't going to be that easy.

"Hey, Reesie, what's that?" Amy asked as Theresa shuffled past her sister's room. "A little black book with all your boyfriends' phone numbers in it?"

"Good one, Amy," Theresa grumbled. She looked in to see her sister sprawled across her bed with her cell phone in one hand and the TV remote in the other. "No, it's a planner."

"A planner? What's up with that? Is my ditzy sister finally trying to get organized?" Amy laughed.

Ditzy. Nice. That was something she hadn't been called yet today. "It's for my homework. And spring carnival," Theresa explained.

"Why do you need a planner for spring carnival?" Amy asked.

"Because I'm in charge of organizing the booths and decorations," Theresa replied. She started to walk away, hoping her sister would leave it at that, but she could never be so lucky.

Amy sprang to her feet and jumped into the hallway. "They put *you* in charge?" she asked, her tone sounding remarkably like Sharon's.

"So?"

"It's just that . . . wow—that's a really important job. I mean, when the judges come around, that's the big thing they're looking at—how well all the booths fit the theme and how well organized everything is. At least that's what Mr. Howell told me when he was a judge my eighth-grade year."

"Mr. Howell is a lunatic," Theresa complained, remembering how upset he'd gotten about her missing homework.

"Oh, yeah," Amy agreed. "He's freakishly neat, but he was right. Amanda Klein was super-organized with all of the decorating—from setting up to taking down—and we won."

"Well, thanks for the pep talk, Ame—I think I'm going to go get started," Theresa said, and she tried to walk away again.

"What's your theme?" Amy persisted.

Theresa stopped and sighed. Why couldn't her sister just ignore her tonight like she did every other night? "It's 3004," she said.

"Three thousand four?" Amy repeated. "That's kind of lame. Who came up with that?"

"I did," Theresa mumbled.

"Oh. Well, I'm sure you'll find a way to make it work."

"Thanks, Amy," Theresa droned. Then she plodded down the hall, wishing there was some way she could erase the last twelve hours and start over again.

When she got into her room, Theresa closed the door and leaned back against it. "Ugh," she groaned. First Sharon and now Amy. Who would be next?

"Izzy!" she whisper-shouted into the air. "Are you in here?"

Theresa waited a minute, then tried again. "Izzy?" Again there was no answer.

"Great," Theresa muttered. "Now I'm imagining

that little people are talking to me at the mall."

"You didn't imagine me," the fairy called.

Theresa's eyes darted around the room. "Where are you?"

"Up here," Izzy shouted. Theresa raised her head and looked at the ceiling just in time to see Izzy floating down with a parachute. Then she clapped, and the next thing Theresa knew, the parachute was gone and Izzy was standing on her desk, dressed in a leather bomber jacket, a white scarf, an old-fashioned pilot's helmet, and flying goggles.

"What in the world are you wearing?" Theresa asked.

"You like it?" Izzy asked, flipping the scarf over her shoulder. "Amelia had an extra uniform in her cockpit, so I—"

"Amelia?" Theresa asked. "As in Amelia Earhart?"

"I had a little free time on my way back here," Izzy said matter-of-factly. "I stopped in to wish her luck on her first solo flight."

Theresa shook her head. "Wait a second," she said. "First you were hiking with Lewis and Clark, and now you've been hanging out with Amelia Earhart?"

"What can I say? I'm a history buff," Izzy said. She clapped again and transformed her flight gear into a long, flowing, patterned skirt, a white tank top, and, once again, Birkenstocks. "There. Are you ready to get down to business?"

Theresa sighed. "I guess," she said. "I just don't know how I'm going to pull this off when nobody believes that I can—including me."

"Ah," Izzy said. "I can help you with that." She clicked her heels, and suddenly a podium appeared in front of her. The little fairy was now sporting a tailored business suit. Her hair was drawn up in a loose bun, and she was wearing horn-rimmed glasses. She leaned forward and spoke into a bunch of microphones like she was giving a press conference. "First, you're going to be realistic," she said, her voice booming through the room.

"Izzy!" Theresa hissed, covering her ears.

"Sorry," Isadora said. "I've never been very good with mikes. Too formal." She waved her hand and the podium disappeared. "Let me try that again. First, you're going to be realistic," she said at a much lower volume.

"What's that supposed to mean?" Theresa asked.

"Well, you just said that nobody believes in you. Is that true?"

"Didn't you just hear my sister?" Theresa replied.

"Yes," Izzy said matter-of-factly. "And I heard that ridiculous girl at the mall, too."

"Sharon," Theresa said.

"Right—the one who needs a good drenching," Izzy replied. "But tell me . . . who else has said they don't believe in you?"

"Well . . ." Theresa said. She chewed the inside of her cheek and thought it over. "There are the kids Sharon was talking to today when she said I was klutzy and disorganized."

Izzy shook her head. "No—that was just Sharon again. You didn't hear whether anyone actually agreed with her or not."

"How do you know that?" Theresa demanded. "You weren't there."

"It was in your file," Izzy explained. "All that stuff I read on that screen?"

"Oh. Well—what about Carrie and Anna? They haven't exactly been cheering me on."

"*No*, but they haven't been knocking you down, either. They're just looking out for you— they're your friends. And if you asked for their help or their support, you know they'd be there for you in a heartbeat."

"I suppose," Theresa said.

"So then really what it comes down to is that two people have questioned your organizational skills, and you're not confident you can pull this off, right?"

Theresa shrugged. "I guess," she said.

"You *guess?*" Izzy said. "Well, I *know*. Trust me." She snapped her fingers, and Theresa's room went pitch-black. The next thing Theresa knew, she was sitting in a folding chair, with a bottle of spring water in one hand and a tub of popcorn in the other.

"Izzy—?" she started, but then suddenly a slide projector clicked on and the words *be realistic* flashed on one of Theresa's bedroom walls.

"So like I said, that's number one," Izzy announced, underscoring the words with an extra-long pointer. "Be realistic. The whole world isn't against you, and nothing horrible is going to happen if your class doesn't win."

"Except that everyone is going to hate me," Theresa said.

"Uh, uh, uh," Izzy said, waving her pointer. "There you go again. Remember—be *realistic*— not *pessimistic*."

Theresa rolled her eyes. It sounded like something her mother would say.

"Now, number two," Izzy went on. She pressed

a clicker that had magically appeared in her hand, and the projector flipped to the next slide.

Theresa read the words that flashed on her wall in bold black letters. "'Break it down'?" she asked. "What's that supposed to mean?"

"It means," Izzy said, gesturing with her pointer as she spoke, "that big tasks can seem overwhelming. But if you break them down into smaller steps and tackle each one individually, they're easier to get done."

Theresa tilted her head. "You mean like when my mom tells me to clean my room. It always seems impossible at first, but then she comes in and helps me put away clothes, then organize my bookshelf, then clear off my desk, and pretty soon it looks a lot better."

"That's exactly what I mean," Izzy said. "And that's what you need to do with this spring carnival thing. Break it down into little pieces instead of trying to tackle the whole thing at once."

"All right, I guess I can try that," Theresa said. She took a sip of the spring water. "What else have you got?"

Izzy smiled. "We're down to the big three," she said. "The most important things to remember. Are you ready?"

Theresa leaned back in her chair and

grabbed a fistful of popcorn. "As ready as I'll ever be," she said.

"All right," Izzy said, and she pressed the clicker again. "Here they are. Number three: Do your best—because that's all you ever can do. Number four," she continued, clicking to the next frame, "ask for help when you need it—because being in charge doesn't mean working alone. And most important, number five—"

Izzy waved her pointer and everything in Theresa's room returned to normal. The lights came up, the projector was gone—even Theresa's tub of popcorn had disappeared.

"Hey, I was eating that," Theresa protested.

"Don't interrupt," Izzy told her. "And number five," she repeated, waving her hands dramatically, "have fun!" On the word *fun*, Izzy pointed both of her index fingers into the air like little guns, and suddenly confetti shot from the ceiling, raining down on a little basket of goodies that had appeared on Theresa's desk.

"What's all this?" Theresa asked, picking out a pack of bubble gum.

"Study supplies," Izzy said. "I wasn't sure what you liked, so I got a little of everything."

Theresa dug through the shredded paper in

the basket and plucked out a small plastic egg. "Silly Putty is a study supply?" she asked.

"Mm-hm." Izzy nodded. "And so are Legos," she said, pointing to a small box at the bottom. "They're both excellent for plotting things out and getting creative ideas."

"And the Slinky?" Theresa asked.

"A reminder to stay flexible."

"What about this?" Theresa said, picking up a miniature satin pillow that looked remarkably like the one Izzy was always hovering on.

"Sometimes you just have to take a break," Izzy said. "That's important, too, you know."

"I guess it is," Theresa said.

"But before you can take a break, you have to start working," Izzy said. "So get out that planner, and let's figure out what you have to do. Do you remember the tips I gave you?"

Theresa closed her eyes and pictured the slide show on her wall. "Be realistic," she said. "Break it down, do your best, ask for help when you need it . . . and have fun."

"Perfect," Izzy congratulated her. "Remember those and you're golden."

Golden, Theresa thought. *Sure. Either that or bright red when I fall flat on my face in front of the whole school.*

CHAPTER
Nine

"Well, you all certainly did a wonderful job coming up with booth ideas," Mrs. Wessex said, motioning to the list that now covered three sections of the chalkboard. Evidently Sharon had been lying when she'd said that people were having a hard time with Theresa's theme. Everyone seemed plenty enthusiastic about it today.

"I told you not to trust her," Izzy said, appearing on Theresa's shoulder.

Theresa chortled, causing Carrie to give her a bewildered look. "What?" she mouthed.

"Nothing," Theresa whispered back. Then she glanced at Izzy.

This time the little fairy was dressed in a long black dress with a white apron and matching bonnet.

Theresa raised one eyebrow at the tiny sprite.

"Plymouth," Izzy said, rubbing her stomach. "Great place for a turkey dinner."

Theresa's jaw dropped and she started to ask Izzy if she was talking about *the* Plymouth—the one where the first Thanksgiving had taken place—but Izzy stopped her.

"Better pay attention," the fairy said. "You're on."

I'm what? Theresa wondered. But she didn't have to wait long to find out.

"Now, Theresa," Mrs. Wessex said. "I was hoping that you could come up front and share some of your decorating ideas with us. And then maybe everyone can help to brainstorm ways to use those ideas in their booths. How does that sound?"

Gulp. "Fine," Theresa said. She stood up and began weaving her way to the front of the class, stepping over, behind, and between all of the fifth graders who were packed into the room.

"Remember the tips!" Izzy whispered in her ear, and then she vanished. But Theresa had a feeling she hadn't gone too far.

"Okay," Theresa began. "Since the theme is 3004, I thought that to start off, we should have two big banners that say, 3004: See What's in Store."

"See what's in store?" Sharon sneered. "Isn't that kind of hokey?" Billy and Jeremy chortled, and it looked like Lauren and Maria were giggling, too.

"Well, it doesn't have to be that, exactly," Theresa said. "I mean, if someone wants to come up with something else, that's fine, too. I just thought it would be good to have banners over the entrances."

"To the gym?" Kimberly asked.

"We can't put stuff over the entrances to the gym," Sharon said. "Only in our area. Which reminds me—do you know which corner we're getting yet? Because if we're in the back, maybe we can use the trampoline for a moon bounce or something."

"That would be awesome," Kimberly said. "Can we, Mrs. Wessex?"

"I'm not sure about that, Kimberly, but right now we need to listen to Theresa and think about our decorations," Mrs. Wessex said. "Theresa—go ahead."

Theresa swallowed hard and tried to regain her train of thought. She didn't usually have trouble talking in front of people. But then again, she didn't usually have Sharon sitting in the front row trying to sabotage her, either.

"So anyway, like I was saying, I think we should use banners to mark the entrances to our area—I didn't mean the entrances to the gym—and we could make those entrances by setting up the booths like this."

Theresa reached into the canvas bag she had brought to school that day and removed a model she'd built out of Legos.

"Uh, hello?" Sharon said. "Legos have been around for a long time, Theresa. I don't think anyone's going to believe they were invented in 3004."

A bunch of students laughed at Sharon's comment, and it took Mrs. Wessex another thirty seconds to get everyone quieted down again. *Why can't she just let me talk?* Theresa wondered.

She was beginning to get frustrated with all of Sharon's comments, but when she looked over at Sharon, her grimace turned into a smile. There, floating just above Sharon's head, was Izzy in a miniature hot air balloon with the words *Inflated by Sharon Ross* written on the front.

Theresa started to giggle, but she managed to stop herself by taking a deep breath.

When she looked at Sharon again, Izzy's hot air balloon was gone. Instead, there were five new ones floating around the room—each with one of Izzy's tips emblazoned on its side: *Be realistic.*

Break it down. Do your best. Ask for help. Have fun.
Theresa read the words and felt her spirits lifting.

Sharon might not think Theresa could handle being in charge of spring carnival, and there might even be a few others in the room who agreed with her, but Theresa knew that she didn't have to let them get to her. And she also knew that she'd worked hard last night getting ready for this meeting. She was doing her best, and that was all anyone could ask of her. And now it was time to have fun.

She cleared her throat, took a deep breath, and got ready. "Okay, so if you take a look at the Legos," Theresa said, holding up her model so everyone could see it, "you'll understand what I mean about the banners. See—we can set up our booths so that our whole area is walled off, like this. And then there can be just two entrances—one at each end. That way it will be really easy to decorate our section and make it feel like its our own space."

"I see what you mean, Theresa," Mrs. Wessex said. "That's rather clever. Usually people just line their booths up along the wall."

"I know," Theresa said. "I was looking at pictures of spring carnival in my sister's old yearbooks last night, and it just seemed like there was a lot of wasted space in the center of the gym. That's what gave me the idea to arrange our area differently."

"We could make arches with balloons," Carrie suggested. "My cousin did that for her prom last year and it looked really neat."

"Hey," Maria said. "I've seen those before. They're really nice."

"Sure, they are—*at proms*," Sharon said.

"I think they'd work okay here, too," Theresa said. "They'd really separate our area, and they'd give us a place to put the banners. And you know—maybe the banners could just say, Welcome to 3004. Then, on the inside of each archway, we could do another set of banners that say, You are now leaving 3004—Please come again. You know, like the way they do town signs?"

"That's a cool idea," Jeremy said. "Then it would be like we had our own town in the gym."

"Hey—that gives me a whole new idea for decorating," Theresa exclaimed suddenly. "Why don't we make it like a town in 3004? All of our booths could be like separate stores of the future." She turned to the list on the chalkboard and started scanning all the ideas.

"Okay, like this. Billy—you and Jeremy are doing something on future vehicles, right? So your booth could look like a futuristic car dealership."

"Cool," Billy and Jeremy said at the same time.

"And Lauren and Maria—you two wanted to do future food, right?"

"Right."

"So how about making your booth into, I don't know . . . Café Neptune or something like that? It could be a restaurant of the future, and you could come up with weird menus and stuff."

"Yeah, I like it," Maria said.

"Me too," Lauren agreed.

"And Matt—you wanted to do something with sports, so your booth could be a futuristic sporting goods store with all kinds of freaky equipment for stuff like . . . crater diving and . . . surfing Saturn's rings."

The classroom started to buzz with excitement as everyone began coming up with more ideas for their futuristic town, and Theresa felt like she was positively glowing. As soon as she'd relaxed and started to have fun, the ideas had just come flying into her head, and now she and all the other fifth graders were really psyched for spring carnival.

"Well, Theresa," Mrs. Wessex said, walking over to her and touching her shoulder gently. "I can see I put the right person in charge. You've done a wonderful job getting us started. Look at how excited everyone is."

Theresa glanced around the room to see everyone smiling and talking about things they could add to their booths. It was so cool to know that she'd been the one to come up with the idea they were all so pumped about.

"Thanks, Mrs. Wessex," Theresa said.

"No—thank you. You've put in a lot of work already," Mrs. Wessex said, "and it shows."

Theresa stared down at her feet. She knew she must be blushing, but it wasn't because she was embarrassed. It was because she was proud.

"Mrs. Wessex? Can I go to the bathroom?" Sharon asked. And that was when Theresa realized that Sharon was the only person in the room who wasn't smiling.

"Certainly, Sharon. Just grab the bathroom pass off my desk," Mrs. Wessex said.

Theresa watched as Sharon plodded over to get the pass and then walked out the door, dragging her feet all the way.

If only there was a way to get Sharon to help instead of trying to make things difficult, Theresa thought. And then, just as one of Izzy's hot air balloons came floating by, she realized that there was.

CHAPTER
Ten

"Theresa—you had such awesome ideas at the class meeting this morning," Anna said as Theresa sat down at the lunch table. "Everyone's been talking about it all day."

"You were so great, Resa!" Carrie agreed. "I can't believe you were worried about being in charge."

"I can," Sharon muttered without looking up from her salad. She'd been sulky and quiet most of the morning, Theresa had noticed. But now it sounded like she was ready to give Theresa a hard time again, which was fine. This time Theresa was ready.

"What do you mean, *you can*?" Anna asked. "Theresa's doing a great job."

"She has good ideas, I'll give her that," Sharon said. "But there's still a lot of work to do, and if Theresa is her usual disorganized self, she could still blow it."

"Sharon!" Carrie said.

"Yo, girls, let's keep it positive," Spence said. "No need to complain, let's refrain from disdain."

"Just say the word and I'll turn her into an emu," Izzy said. She had appeared out of nowhere, this time wearing a suit of armor and riding a black horse—fresh from the Middle Ages, no doubt. As her horse reared up, Izzy pointed her sword toward Sharon, ready to work her magic.

"No!" Theresa shouted, sending everyone at the table into shocked silence. "I mean, no—don't get upset with Sharon. She's right."

Carrie and Anna gawked at Theresa like she was crazy. "She is?" they said.

"I am?" Sharon asked.

"She's what?" Izzy demanded, whirling around on her stallion.

"Sharon's right," Theresa repeated. "There's still a lot of work to be done to get everything ready for spring carnival, and I'm not the most organized person around, so—I'm going to need a lot of help staying on top of stuff."

For a second everyone just looked around

the table, not quite sure what to say. Then Spence leaned forward.

"Okay—shoot. What do you need? You got your posse right here, ready to pitch in."

"My *posse*?" Theresa asked.

"Sure," Spence said. "Me, Matt, Anna, Carrie—just tell us what you need."

"Okay," Theresa said. She flipped her planner to one of the back sections, where she had made a neat list of all the things that needed to be done right away. "I need someone to check on the cost of making those balloon archways," she said.

"Got it," Carrie said, raising her hand. "My mom's taking me to get new sneakers this afternoon, and the party store is right next door."

"Great," Theresa said. "All right. I also need someone to see if the local grocery will donate paper cups and napkins for all the people who plan to serve food."

"I'm there," Matt volunteered. "I can stop in on my way to the skate park this afternoon."

"Excellent. Thanks," Theresa said, penciling Matt's name in next to that task. "Okay, the next one's a big one. Sharon," Theresa said, turning to face her, "I'd really be psyched if you could do it."

Sharon drew back slightly and scrunched her eyebrows together. "What is it?" she asked a little suspiciously.

"It's the decorating committee. I need someone to make sure there are plenty of people to help put up all the decorations in the morning, and then I need another crew to help take them all down at the end of the day. It's really important that I have someone organized and responsible in charge of this, and, well—you were the first person I thought of."

"Really?" Sharon asked.

"Yeah, really," Theresa said, and she meant it. As mean as Sharon could be when she didn't get her way, she really was one of the most organized people Theresa knew. And she took her responsibilities seriously, too.

"Well . . ." Sharon looked around at all the others, who were anxiously awaiting her answer. "Okay. I guess I could do that."

"Awesome!" Theresa said. "Thanks, Sharon. With you in charge of getting stuff set up, I just know everything's going to run smoothly."

"I'll make sure there aren't any problems," Sharon said.

Perfect, Theresa thought. *Just what I was hoping for.* She shot a smug smile at Isadora, who had lost the knight costume and was now sitting cross-legged on Sharon's dinner roll.

"Nicely done," Izzy said. "But I still think she'd make a good emu."

For the next week and a half everyone worked tirelessly on their booths. The decorating committee had met several times to work on the large banners welcoming everyone to the fifth-grade area and signposts to point people to all the different "stores." Lauren and Maria said they'd stayed up until midnight one night working on the menus for their space café. And Matt Dana had held a pizza party over the weekend and invited a ton of people to come help him turn used sports equipment into revolutionary new gear for sports like galaxy surfing and black-hole diving.

By the night before spring carnival, Theresa could barely contain her excitement.

"There's going to be a clothing store called Universal Cool that Kimberly and a few others have been working on," she said as she piled salad onto her plate. "They've been to every secondhand shop and fabric store in the state, picking up weird stuff to use—old prom dresses that they've altered to look like clothes you'd see on *Star Trek* or something."

"That sounds interesting," Mrs. Allen said, passing the potatoes to Theresa.

"Yeah, and Ryan Woods and Melissa Stone painted this space scene on a huge piece of plywood and cut out two circles so people can stick their heads in to make it look like their faces are on the bodies of astronauts floating outside a space station."

"Jeez, Theresa, take a breath," Amy said.

"She's just excited, Amy," Mr. Allen said. "Your sister has been working hard, and all her hard work is about to pay off."

Theresa shot her sister a smug look while her parents weren't looking.

"You're still not going to win," Amy said.

"You don't know that," Theresa retorted. "We've got all kinds of fun booths—Jessica Foster made a game called 3004: What Would You Be? where people throw darts at balloons, and inside each balloon there's a little card describing a career in the year 3004. She has everything from Milky Way movie star and prime minister of Venus to lifeguard at Club Mercury and celebrity dog walker on Pluto."

Amy rolled her eyes and shrugged to show

just how unimpressed she was.

"That's what I'd want to be," said Theresa's little brother, Nicky. "I like dogs."

"You'd be an excellent dog walker, sweetie," said Mrs. Allen. "Amy—take some salad. You haven't been eating enough vegetables lately." Theresa plunked a bite of salmon into her mouth and watched as Amy once again rolled her eyes. "Irritated" seemed to be one of the only expressions she could manage since she'd turned sixteen.

"Look, Reesie," Amy said as she began scooping lettuce and cucumbers onto her plate. She avoided everything else in the salad—tomatoes, yellow peppers, carrots, anything that wasn't green. "I'm not saying that your class hasn't worked hard or that your area won't have cool booths—I'm just telling you not to get your hopes up. Fifth graders are the bottom of the heap, and heap bottoms don't win spring carnival."

Theresa snorted. "That shows what you know," she said. She sat silently for a few minutes, picking at her food, then finally tossed her napkin onto the table. "May I be excused?" she asked, turning to her parents. "I still have to check on a few things for tomorrow."

"Theresa—you've barely eaten," Mrs. Allen protested.

"I know, but I'm not hungry." She glared at Amy and added, "I've lost my appetite. Besides, I need to call the party store to make sure they're all set to deliver the balloon arches, and they close at six-thirty."

Mrs. Allen glanced at Theresa's father, who frowned.

"Please," Theresa begged, giving them her best smile. Mr. Allen held his frown for a few more seconds, then cocked his head and shrugged.

"All right," Mrs. Allen said. "But just this once. And I expect you to have a healthy snack before bed."

"I will," Theresa said, rushing over to her mother and wrapping her arms around her neck. "Thanks, Mom. Thanks, Dad." Then she scurried out of the dining room and up to her bedroom.

"You really should eat more, you know," a small voice said when Theresa reached for her planner. "Big day tomorrow."

"I know, I just—" Theresa stopped short. Izzy was standing on her desk wearing a tattered white silk shirt with billowing arms and black pants with torn cuffs. She was barefoot, and she had a bright red silk scarf tied around her waist and a short black one on her head. Large gold hoop earrings dangled from her ears, and in her hand she brandished a short sword.

"Nice outfit," Theresa said. "But I didn't think pirates let women on their ships."

"Some did," Izzy answered. "Ever hear of Anne Bonney or Mary Read?"

"No."

"Well, then, you should look them up sometime. Remarkable women, even if they were criminals. I was just chatting with them about what it was like to be a woman pirate—interesting stuff. So what are you up to?"

Theresa chuckled. "Nothing that adventurous," she said, unzipping her planner and flipping to the page where she'd copied down the number of the party store. "Just making sure everything's ready for tomorrow." She punched the numbers on the cordless phone she'd snagged from the hallway table and waited. As she did, Izzy was advancing and retreating across her desk, practicing various fencing moves she'd picked up on one of her journeys.

"Parties Unlimited, this is Beth speaking, how can I help you?" a voice finally said.

"Hi, my name is Theresa Allen, and I was just calling to check on some balloon archways that I ordered."

"Hold on one minute, please," the clerk instructed her. "Ah, yes. Theresa Allen. Two ten-foot archways, silver and white balloons . . . mm-hm. Everything seems to be in order. Those will be ready for delivery next Friday."

"*Next* Friday?" Theresa asked. "You mean *this* Friday, right? As in tomorrow?"

There was a brief silence on the line. "No, I mean *next* Friday—as in the twentieth. That's the date they were ordered for."

Theresa's jaw dropped. There had to be some mistake. "Are you sure?" she asked the clerk. "Because I placed that order myself, and I can't imagine I gave you the wrong date."

"I'm looking at the original order slip here," replied the clerk, "and it clearly says you need them for the twentieth."

Izzy had stopped practicing her sword fighting and was now staring at Theresa. "What's wrong?" she asked, but Theresa just waved for her to be quiet.

"Well," Theresa said, her mind reeling, "can you change that? Because I need them for a spring carnival competition that's happening tomorrow—not next Friday."

At the other end of the phone the clerk laughed. "Oh, sweetheart. I'm sorry. Balloon arches take at least a day to put together, and yours haven't even been started."

"But there's been a mistake," Theresa said. "I ordered them for the thirteenth—I know I did. Can't you rush them or something? Or, I don't know, get someone to come in and put them together tonight?"

"I'm sorry, but—"

"Isn't there *anything* you can do?" Theresa pleaded.

The clerk paused. "I can cancel the order so you won't have to pay for it," she offered. Theresa's mouth hung open. This couldn't be happening.

"But you're the ones who made the mistake," she protested, "not me."

Theresa flipped madly through her planner, searching for the calendar section, where she'd written down the confirmation number for her order. *February, March, April—there.* All at once, Theresa's eyes popped. The space for Friday the thirteenth was blank. One row below it, however, in the box for the twentieth, she had written the word *balloons* with a confirmation number and placed a little check mark next to it.

"Oh, no," Theresa moaned. "It *was* my fault."

"Excuse me?" the clerk asked.

"I'm sorry," Theresa said. "You're right. But please just . . . go ahead and cancel the order. If I can't get the archways tomorrow, I don't need them."

"Okay. I'll take care of that for you right away," the clerk said cheerfully. "Is there anything else I can help you with this evening?"

Sure, an escape plan, Theresa thought. "No, no thanks," she said. Theresa hung up the phone and felt her heart sink to the floor.

"What's going on?" Izzy asked. She put her sword back in its sheath, then snapped her fingers and lost the pirate gear altogether, changing into slightly more casual clothing—a pair of tan drawstring pants, a crocheted top, and her faithful Birkenstocks.

"I've ruined the spring carnival," Theresa said, dropping her head onto her desk.

"What do you mean?" Izzy asked.

"The balloon archways," Theresa groaned. "The entryway to our area. I messed it up. Now we don't have anything. No place to put the welcome signs, no way to make our area stand out, and no chance of winning. And it's all my fault."

"What are you talking about?" Izzy asked.

"I ordered the balloons for the wrong date," Theresa said, her head still resting on her desk.

"Sharon was right—Mrs. Wessex did blow our chances of winning when she put me in charge. Now we're going to lose, and I'm never going to hear the end of it from Amy. Even worse, no one in my class is ever going to trust me to be in charge of anything important ever again. I wish I could disappear from the face of the earth."

Theresa had lain there on her desk wallowing for another thirty seconds when suddenly it occurred to her that Izzy was being uncharacteristically quiet. She raised her head ever so slightly to see the tiny sprite standing there with her arms folded across her chest, glowering at Theresa.

"What?" Theresa asked, uncertain what she'd done to earn such a harsh look.

"Are you quite finished?" Izzy asked. "Anything else you want to throw in there? Maybe, 'The world's going to end, and it's all my fault'? Or how about, 'I'm the worst person on the face of the earth and no one's ever going to talk to me again. I might as well find an underground cave and live there for the rest of my life.'" Isadora shook her head. "I should turn *you* into an emu."

"*What?*" Theresa demanded, sitting up straight.

"At least Sharon doesn't give up. She didn't get to be in charge of decorations, but she's been busting her butt just the same. But you—" Izzy stared at the ceiling in frustration. "One little thing goes wrong and it's, 'Poor me, nothing ever goes my way, blah blah blah.'"

"I don't sound like that," Theresa said.

"No—you sound worse," Izzy replied matter-of-factly.

"Well, what do you want me to do? Jump up and down and cheer about the fact that I've messed everything up?"

"*No,*" Isadora said. "I want you to deal with it."

Theresa slumped forward again. "Oh, I see," she said sarcastically. "You want me to be realistic, break it down, do my best, ask for help, and have fun, huh? Fine. Here goes—realistically, I've messed up, and there's nothing to break down because we have no archways. I've been doing my best, but it obviously isn't good enough, and nobody can help me now because it's too late. As for having fun, it's hard to do when I've just proved to my sister and the rest of the world that I really am the disorganized idiot they all thought I was."

Isadora shook her head. "An emu would be too good for you."

"Aaargh!" Theresa roared. "Don't you get it, Izzy? It's over. I messed up, and there's nothing I can do about it."

"Nothing, huh? Do you suppose that's what Lewis and Clark said when they were cold and hungry and stuck in the middle of a mountain range? 'Gee, we've really messed up, and there's nothing we can do about it. We might as well quit right here.' Do you think that's what they did?"

Theresa sighed.

"Of course they didn't!" Izzy answered herself. "They kept going, and eventually they made it through. And what about Amelia Earhart? When people told her aviation was for men, did she give up? No way! She proved them wrong. She saved up enough money to buy her own plane and flew it right across the Atlantic Ocean!

"And how about the Pilgrims? Their first winter in America was really tough, but when spring finally came, did they just hop back on their boat and sail away? No—they dug in and prepared themselves better the second time around, and the next winter was a little bit easier."

Theresa folded her arms across her chest and scowled at the little fairy. True, none of those people had given up, but none of them had been dealing with balloon arches, had they?

Izzy took a few steps closer to Theresa and looked her in the eyes. "You say you're being realistic when you say there's nothing you can do, but it doesn't sound very realistic to me," Isadora said. "You still have fourteen hours before it's time to set up for spring carnival, which is plenty of time if you break down what you need to do and ask for help from—what did Spence call them?"

"My posse," Theresa grumbled.

"That's right—your posse." Isadora smiled. "I do like that boy. He has a way with words."

Theresa chortled in spite of herself. "He does," she agreed, almost smiling. Then she remembered the archways. "Look, Izzy, I know you're trying to help me out and everything, but I just don't see what I can do at this point. It's too late for the party store to make our arches, and that's not something I can do on my own even if all my friends do pitch in and help."

Izzy jumped into the air and glided to the top of Theresa's lamp, perching on the rim so that she was face-to-face with Theresa. "You remember those tips I gave you?"

"Yes, but—"

"Well, I left one out."

Theresa narrowed her eyes. "What is it?" she asked wearily. She was pretty sure Izzy didn't have a tip that would help her now unless it was: *Ask your magical fairy friend to whip up a few balloon archways out of thin air.*

"Capitalize on your strengths," Izzy said.

Theresa craned her neck to lean in closer to the fairy. "What does that mean?"

"It means that everyone has something they're good at—a strength of some sort. So when you're working on a project like this, you should always find your strengths and use them."

"I still don't see what you mean," Theresa said. "I don't even know what my strengths are."

"Yes, you do," Izzy said. "You already told me once."

"I did?"

"Mm-hm. At the mall. When Spence came to you for advice. Do you remember what you said to me?"

Theresa squinted, trying to remember. "Be quiet?" she guessed.

"No-o," Izzy replied. "You told me the organization was hard for you, but the ideas came easy."

"Oh, right. I guess I did," Theresa said. "But how's that supposed to help me now? I don't need more booth ideas—I need a balloon archway."

"So come up with a way to make one," Izzy said. "Or come up with another idea for an entryway. You said it yourself—*the ideas come easy.* You're creative, Theresa—and you're a quick thinker. So stop whining about the archways that you're not going to get and come up with something else."

Theresa sat back in her chair and folded her arms across her chest. Everyone was expecting balloon-lined entryways. They were bound to be disappointed with anything else she came up with at the last minute. *Unless* . . .

"Hey, Izzy—pass me that pencil," Theresa said. The fairy waved a finger and floated the pencil over to Theresa. "Thanks," Theresa said, snagging it out of the air. "I wonder," Theresa muttered, making a quick sketch on one of the pieces of graph paper in her planner. "If we had Ms. Gilbert let down a few of the rings and tied a rope here. . ." She made a few more lines on her graph paper, then sat back to look at it.

Slowly a smile crept onto Theresa's face. "You know, Izzy, that just might work. But it's going to take the whole posse to pull it off."

CHAPTER
Eleven

"There—how's that?" Sharon asked, stapling the last of the silver balloons onto the makeshift archway Theresa had designed just last night.

"It looks great, Sharon," Theresa gushed. "Thank you so much for getting everyone here early to make this work."

"No problem," Sharon said. "It was easy. Everyone was willing to come in when they heard what happened with the order."

Theresa pressed her eyes closed. "I still can't believe I had the wrong date," she said.

"Don't sweat it," Sharon said. Theresa stared at her, wide-eyed. She'd expected Sharon to make a snide comment about how disorganized she was or what a ditz she was, but she certainly hadn't expected Sharon to be supportive.

"Really?" Theresa asked.

"Sure. I mean, it wasn't the smartest thing you've ever done. . . ."

That's more like it, Theresa thought.

"But still, you did a good job pulling everything together. The fifth-grade area looks great, and you know—" Sharon stepped back to admire the entryway. "I actually think this looks better than the one we would have gotten from the party store. The streamers make it look more complete."

Theresa gazed at the curtain of white streamers dangling from the ceiling, each one with a shiny balloon attached to the end. She and the other members of the decorating crew had created entryways by suspending ropes like clotheslines at each end of their area. Each rope was about fifteen feet long and hung about ten feet above the floor.

Once these "clotheslines" were up, Theresa and the others had cut lengths of white streamers to hang straight down from the ropes. The streamers at the outer edges hung all the way to the floor, but as they worked their way inward, the decorators had made each successive streamer a little shorter so that the ones in the middle were only about a foot and a half long. The overall effect was that of an archway, and to finish it off, they'd attached silver and white balloons to the ends of the streamers, turning it into a balloon archway.

"It does look pretty good," Theresa agreed. "How's everything else coming along?"

"I think we're all set," Sharon said, "but I'm going to walk through one last time just to be sure."

"Good idea," Theresa said. "Thanks again, Sharon."

"Anytime," Sharon called over her shoulder. Theresa took a few steps back to admire both entryways. Across the top of each were huge banners that read, Welcome to 3004. It really did look incredible.

Theresa sighed. Izzy had been right. Once she'd stopped whining and started focusing, she'd been able to come up with a solution to her archway problem. And by breaking down the tasks and asking for help from her friends, she'd managed to make it work. Carrie had scored the extra streamers and balloons, Spence had come through with the ropes, Matt and Anna had each brought stepladders, and Sharon had called everyone on the setup crew to get them in a half hour earlier. The whole posse had come through.

And the fifth-grade area, with its enclosed futuristic town, really stood out. All of the rest of the classes had set up their booths the traditional way—backed up against the walls. A few booths in each section were set in closer to the center of the floor, but the fifth grade was the only class that had turned their area into a contained space, and the effect was amazing.

Theresa walked through the rear arch and found herself facing the Astro Gym. As it turned out, Mrs. Wessex had been able to arrange for the fifth graders to use the trampoline after all.

Sharon had worked with Lesley Fine to decorate its edges with gray moon-rock pillows. They'd also created a storefront made from cardboard and streamers and a big sign inviting people inside to try the most technologically advanced exercise machine of 3004—the moon bounce.

The next store in their futuristic town was the W^2 Music Emporium, where people could check out bands in the year 3004, as designed by Spence and Carrie, aka W^2—for Willis and Weingarten.

"This looks great, you guys," Theresa said as she checked out some of the weird album covers Carrie had designed and the phony song titles and lyrics that Spence had come up with. "And I love your alien costume, Spence."

Following Theresa's suggestion, Spence had come dressed as a famous alien rapper who was getting ready for his first Earth concert tour. He had two heads, five eyes, and a spiked, dragonlike tail. All day long he planned to challenge people to freestyle battles. Carrie was ready to hand out candy and dollar-store prizes to anyone who could outrhyme him.

"Yo, Theresa—you want to be my first opponent?" Spence asked. His voice was muffled by his costume, but it didn't seem to affect his ability to rhyme. "We'll have a freestyle battle. / You can shake, roll, and rattle / and I'll rap until the cattle come home."

Theresa laughed and shook her head. "I think you just won, Spence. Carrie, you're going to be holding that loot all day, you know."

"I know," Carrie said. "Maybe I should just give it out to anyone who dares to challenge him."

"That might be a better idea," Theresa agreed.

As she continued her walk, she passed Todd Metcalf's Surreal Estate, where people could view models of rental condos on Mars, and Billy and Jeremy's Used Car Lot, where people could test drive a "space car" that Billy and Jeremy had built from spare wood and old appliance parts.

Theresa had been a little wary when they'd

first brought it in, but it actually worked really well. It had a wooden frame with wings and all kinds of dials and controls on the inside. Then Billy and Jeremy had set up a big TV in front of it and put in a video with footage taken from a helicopter camera so that it seemed like the car was actually flying through the sky.

There were tons of other booths, too, like Lauren and Maria's Intergalactic Café and XTreme Planet, the sporting goods store Matt had set up with a couple of his buddies. Anna was running a bakery, where she and a bunch of others were holding cakewalks, only they were calling them "moonwalks." And instead of walking away with a cake, the winner received a MoonPie.

Overall, the fifth-grade area looked amazing. There were silver and white balloons everywhere, and everyone had done a great job making their booths look futuristic and cutting-edge. Theresa was psyched. It felt like they actually had a shot at winning.

"Hey—have you checked out the other areas yet?" a tiny voice said in her ear. Theresa turned to see Izzy wearing astronaut gear and hovering next to Theresa's head in a mini space shuttle.

"I thought you said you were a *history* buff,"

Theresa said, keeping her mouth as still as possible when she spoke.

Izzy tapped a patch on her bright orange uniform, which bore the initials *S. R.* "I borrowed this suit from Sally Ride, the first woman in space," she said. "She was a very important part of history indeed. Besides, I wanted to support your whole future theme, so showing up in a stagecoach or a Model T didn't seem appropriate."

"Good point," Theresa said.

"Thanks," Izzy said. "So—have you checked out all the other classes' themes?" she asked for the second time.

"No, but—"

"Well, I have," Izzy said, "and you have absolutely no competition. The eighth grade did Hollywood, yawn, and the sixth graders just have a whole bunch of carnival booths and a couple of bales of hay. I think it's supposed to be a county fair."

"What about the seventh grade?" Theresa asked.

Izzy pressed her eyes closed and shook her head. "That one you have to see for yourself. Come on!"

"Izzy, I—" Theresa started, but it was no use.

Izzy's spaceship had already whizzed ahead and out through the far archway. *"Oo-kay,"* Theresa said with a sigh. "I guess I'll go check out the other areas."

She followed Izzy's path out of the fifth-grade section and across the gym to where the seventh grade was set up. "Uh-oh," she said as soon as she saw their sign.

"Can you believe it?" Izzy said, pointing to one of the booths. "They're all over the place."

Theresa gazed at all the booths. The seventh grade had chosen fairy tales as their theme, and as a result, there were little pictures of fairies on just about everything in their area. But they weren't fairies like Isadora, with baseball hats and hiking boots and astronaut suits and Birkenstocks. No—they were all glittery, winged fairies with short skirts and magic wands. They were—

"Cute little Barbie dolls flitting about in short skirts and butterfly wings. Your school is infested with them," Izzy groaned. "But that's not even the worst part."

Theresa was sure she was going to regret it, but she had to ask. "What is?"

"The stories!" Izzy shouted directly in Theresa's ear.

"Man, it's a good thing no one else can hear you," Theresa muttered, rubbing her temples. "You're not going to transmogrify anybody, are you?"

"Of course not," Izzy said. "Not that they don't deserve it."

Theresa coughed to suppress a smile. Then she cleared her throat. "Wait a second—I get why you're upset about the fairies, but what's wrong with the stories?"

"Isn't it obvious?" Izzy asked. "Look around. What do you see?"

Theresa scanned the booths. They looked fine to her. There was one based on Little Red Riding Hood, one next to that about Snow White, and one farther down with Sleeping Beauty. Theresa also saw the Three Little Pigs, the Three Billy Goats Gruff, and Goldilocks and the Three Bears, among others.

"Well?" Izzy demanded. "Don't you see?"

"See what?" Theresa asked.

Izzy shook her head. "I'll spell it out for you—they're calling these stories *fairy* tales, right?"

"Right."

"So where are the fairies?" Izzy demanded. "Not one of these stories actually has *a fairy*!"

"They don't?" Theresa glanced at all of the nearby booths again and thought it over. "Wow, you're right—they don't. Huh. That's weird. I wonder why we call them fairy tales."

"I have no idea," Izzy said, "but these drawings must be dealt with."

"*Izzy,*" Theresa said, "what are you planning to do?"

"Improve them," Izzy said.

"Izzy—you can't," Theresa told her. "You may not like the booths, but the seventh grade worked hard to make them. You can't just change them around. And besides, they have to be judged for the contest—*without* your improvements."

"Fine," Izzy said. "So I'll wait. But mark my words—those butterfly-winged babes are going down." She glanced at something over Theresa's shoulder. "And soon, too," she added.

"What do you mean?" Theresa asked.

"I mean, here come the judges. They just finished looking at your area."

"They—*what?* How do you know?"

"Because," Isadora said. "They just came out through one of your archways smiling and taking notes, and they're headed this way next."

"Smiling? They were smiling?" Theresa said. "I have to go find out how it went."

Theresa started running toward her class's area, then stopped and turned back to the fairy. "Don't touch anything—okay?"

"I won't," Izzy assured her. "I promise." But there was something about the smile on her face that made Theresa just a little bit nervous.

CHAPTER
Twelve

"I'm so nervous, my knees are shaking," Theresa said.

"Me too," said Anna.

"Me three," added Carrie.

The three girls clasped hands and stared at the front of the gym, where the three judges— Mrs. Hendrickson, the music teacher; Ms. Hamlin, the art teacher; and Mr. Howell—were getting ready to announce this year's spring carnival winner.

According to Carrie, Spence, Anna, Matt, and Sharon, things had gone really well with the judges. They'd stopped at nearly every booth in the fifth-grade area to tell the students what a nice job they'd done, and Mr. Howell had even taken a minute to try to outrhyme Spence.

Of course he'd lost—he'd gotten stuck trying

to rhyme his own name, at which point Spence had jumped in with, "Yo, Mr. Howell / don't throw in the towel. / Your name rhymes with *owl* and *dowel* and *foul.*"

All three judges had laughed and congratulated Spence on his victory, and Carrie had offered them all lollipops just for stopping by. They'd declined, saying they weren't accepting candy or prizes from anyone until the judging was done, but Ms. Hamlin, the art teacher, had said she'd be back later to win one from them, which seemed like a good sign.

Anna said Ms. Hamlin had even commented on the archways, saying they were "much better than those gaudy ones people buy at the party store." And according to Sharon, all three judges had told her that "Welcome to 3004" was the best fifth-grade area they'd ever seen.

Now that it was time for the judges to announce their decision, Theresa found herself replaying that comment over and over in her head. It sounded promising, but then again, the fifth grade had never won spring carnival before. So being the best fifth-grade area ever might not mean all that much.

"Could I have everyone's attention, please?" Ms. Hamlin said into the microphone. She didn't have to ask twice. As full of excitement as the gymnasium was, everyone had gone silent the moment she'd started to speak.

Theresa gripped her friends' hands tighter, and they both squeezed back.

"Thank you," Ms. Hamlin went on. "On behalf of Mr. Howell, Mrs. Hendrickson, and myself, I'd like to say that we were impressed with all of your hard work. I think you all deserve a round of applause."

On the word *applause*, the gymnasium erupted with shouts, whistles, and tons of clapping. Everyone was obviously pretty wound up about the competition—so much so that Theresa could almost feel the tension flowing through her veins. She stopped applauding and reclasped Anna's and Carrie's hands in order to keep her own from shaking.

"All right," Ms. Hamlin said as the noise died down. "This is the moment you've all been waiting for. Choosing one winner is always difficult—especially when everyone has put in such a good effort. But there was one class that really stood out this year, and that class was . . ."

Ms. Hamlin paused for dramatic effect, smiling out at the crowd. Theresa felt her heart pounding in her chest and her mouth going dry.

"Who?" she murmured quietly, unable to contain her excitement. "Who is it?"

"For the first time in ECS history . . . the fifth grade!" Ms. Hamlin finished.

A roar went up all around Theresa as her classmates began jumping up and down, screaming and high-fiving one another.

"We did it!" they were yelling out. And then people started congratulating Theresa personally.

"Awesome theme, Theresa!"

"You rule, Allen!"

"Go get the award, Theresa! Go get the award!"

Theresa looked up at the stage, where all three judges were applauding and Ms. Russell, the principal, was holding a plaque and eyeing the fifth-grade group expectantly.

"Theresa," Mrs. Wessex called from the side of the gym. "Go ahead—go up and accept the award."

Theresa's eyes bugged out. Mrs. Wessex wanted *her* to go up there?

"Yeah, Theresa," Anna said. "Go get it."

"Go, Resa!" Carrie called, grinning and clapping excitedly.

Theresa could hardly believe that everyone wanted her to be the one to accept the award for the fifth grade. But after being told so many times, her legs began to move automatically, and she found herself moving toward the stage as if she were in a dream.

She was halfway to the stage before she even realized what she was doing, and it was then that a thought occurred to her. She glanced up at the stage, where Ms. Russell was patiently waiting, and held up her index finger. "Just a minute," she called, although it was doubtful the principal could hear her over all the applause and chatter that was still going on. Even so, Theresa knew what she needed to do.

She ran back to the fifth-grade group and grabbed Carrie and Anna, Spence, Matt, and Sharon. "You guys come up, too," she said. "None of this would have happened without all of your help."

"No way, Tee," Spence said. "This is all about you—it's your moment of glory."

Theresa put her hands on her hips and grinned. "I want you to come, too, and that's the end of the story," she said.

"You go, Resa!" Carrie giggled, and everyone else laughed, too. Then, with a little more coaxing from Theresa, they all headed up to the stage together.

"Nice work, ladies and gentlemen," Ms.

Russell said as she placed the plaque—which had yet to be engraved—in Theresa's hands.

"Thank you, Ms. Russell," Theresa said. Then she hoisted the plaque above her head for the whole fifth grade to see. Once again the crowd exploded with clapping and cheering, and Theresa couldn't help laughing out of sheer joy.

She looked out at all of her peers, so thrilled to become the first fifth grade ever to win spring carnival, and smiled. Then she scanned the rest of the audience and was surprised to see that people in all the other grades were still clapping and cheering, too. Apparently everyone thought the fifth grade had deserved to win, and as Theresa examined the other areas from the vantage point of the stage, she could see that their area truly did stand out.

She was just about to lower the plaque and turn to leave the stage when something in the seventh-grade area caught her eye. *Oh, no,* she thought, squinting to get a better look. There, floating on her pillow in midair, was Izzy. And behind her was a construction crew, complete with scaffolding, working on the seventh-grade sign that stated their theme: Fairy-Tale Land.

Theresa forced one last smile to the crowd, turned around and shook Ms. Russell's hand, thanking her again, and then walked off the stage. As she and the others returned to the fifth-grade area, everyone began giving Theresa high fives and congratulating her, but all Theresa wanted to do was check on Izzy.

"Could you take over for me here?" she asked, handing the plaque to Sharon. "I need to . . . use the bathroom."

"Sure," Sharon said. She gladly accepted the plaque and held it up again so that the whole fifth grade could get a look at it. And as all of her friends started cheering again, Theresa rushed away, booking it to the seventh-grade section of the gym.

When she got there, Izzy, the pillow, and all the scaffolding was gone. "Izzy?" Theresa whispered. "Where are you?" She hunted around for the fairy for a moment, but her eyes stopped when she saw the seventh grade's sign.

At first Theresa gasped. Then she clapped a hand to her mouth and laughed out loud. True to her word, Izzy hadn't touched a thing, but the construction crew she'd conjured up had altered the image of the fairy completely.

Instead of the wispy winged creature with the short fitted dress, star-tipped wand, and cute blond ponytail, the fairy now looked remarkably like . . . Izzy. The way she'd looked when Theresa had first met her.

She had long brown braids, a Red Sox cap, cargo shorts, and hiking boots, and now the sign read: Fairy-Tale Land—Where Fairies Are People, Too.

Theresa shook her head and grinned. "Okay, Izzy," she said quietly. "You can come out now. I'm not mad. I think it's a big improvement." She stepped closer and looked all around the sign, but there was still no Izzy. Then she saw it.

Down on the floor, just below the spot where Izzy had been relaxing on her pillow, Theresa saw something silver and shiny. She stooped to pick it up and realized that it was the fairy ornament from the top of her pen—only now, instead of wings, the fairy was wearing a baseball hat. And the wand that she'd been holding was gone, too. In its place was simply a small silver hoop. Theresa smiled when she saw it, knowing immediately what it was meant for.

She brought the little fairy charm to her lips and gave it a quick kiss. "Thanks, Izzy," she whispered. "I'll remember all of your tips."

As she was attaching the fairy to her charm bracelet, Theresa noticed that something was written on its back. She flipped it over and read:
Ask for help, do your best, and have fun.

"Especially the big three," she added. Then she clipped the fairy onto her bracelet and headed back to the fifth-grade area to find her friends. They had an ice cream party to prepare for.

"Well, you did it," Amy said later that night. She was standing in Theresa's bedroom doorway.

Theresa looked up from the book she was reading. "I told you we could," she replied with great satisfaction.

"What did you do, bribe the judges?"

"Amy!" Theresa said. She closed her book and sat up on her bed.

"I was only kidding, Reesie. Jeez."

"Maybe you were this time," Theresa said, "but you weren't before. All those times that you said we didn't have a shot and that I'd mess everything up if I was involved, you meant it."

"I meant *some* of it," Amy admitted.

Theresa scowled and folded her arms across her chest.

"Come on, Reesie, don't take everything so seriously. I'm your big sister. I'm supposed to give you a hard time—it builds character."

Theresa remained silent. She cocked her head and continued to glare at her sister.

"And besides, I really didn't think you had a shot at winning. The—"

"See!" Theresa shouted. "There you go again. You think—"

"Dial it back a notch, Reesie," Amy interrupted. "If you'd let me finish, I was going to say that I didn't think you had a shot at winning because the fifth grade never does."

"You mean the fifth grade never *did*," Theresa corrected her.

"Whatever," Amy said, but she was smiling just a tiny bit. "Look, I came in here to say congratulations, but now I'm not so sure I want to."

"So don't," Theresa said, giving her a tiny smile back.

"Fine, I won't." Amy turned and walked away.

Theresa pulled her legs underneath her and sat cross-legged on her bed for a moment, her hands resting on her knees, palms up. *So Amy came in to congratulate me,* she thought, her lips curving into a smile. *Maybe I'll meditate about that for a few minutes.*

She was just beginning to understand why Izzy enjoyed sitting that way so much when something hit her on the side of the head. It was Amy's pillow.

"Amy! What are you doing?" Theresa asked.

Her sister stood a few feet away from her, grinning. "Pillow fight?" she asked playfully.

Theresa smiled. She and Amy had had pillow fights all the time when they were younger, but it had been at least two years since their last one. "You're on," Theresa said. She rolled back on her bed, grabbed her pillow, and walloped her sister on the side.

"Ooh—I'll get you for that one," Amy said, giggling, and then she and Theresa proceeded to thwack each other until they both fell on the floor, laughing.

It's not exactly "Congratulations," Theresa thought, lying in a heap with her older sister, *but it will do.*